SURVIVING MIDDLE SCHOOL

AN INTERACTIVE STORY FOR BOYS

SURVIVING MIDDLE SCHOOL

AN INTERACTIVE STORY FOR BOYS

DAVE MCGRAIL

Crebblehawk Press | New York, NY

Crebblehawk Press
New York, New York

ISBN-13: 978-0692062630
ISBN-10: 0692062637
LCCN: 2018901044

Cover Design and Illustrations by Joaquin Jutt

Printed in the United States of America

To Lauren Somethingorother

Preface

To the kids:

In real life, you are bound to face many of the dilemmas depicted in this book. Some of them will be fleeting and possibly fun to mull over; others will be more serious. I hope you will talk them through with your friends, your school counselors, and, yes, even your parents.

To the parents of boys who are about to make the leap to middle school:

Buckle up.

It's your first day of middle school. Last school year was a breeze. You got good grades, were invited to tons of birthday parties, and set a new personal record when you avoided getting punched in the arm for four straight months. Middle school will be more of the same, except better. Right?

Maybe, maybe not.

Just before you walk out the door, your mom kisses you on the head and tells you to "Jeter it up" this year. She has a bizarre habit of turning athletes into verbs, and you know she's alluding to Derek Jeter's legendary work ethic, integrity, and success. But part of you wonders if, on this big day, her encouragement is more like a jinx.

An hour later, your mom's words still lingering in the air, you enter the school courtyard and spot a group of about thirty boys and a handful of girls standing in a circle. The atmosphere is electric—there is a collective *buzz* emanating from the crowd.

Standing on the outside of the circle, craning his neck for a better view, is Adam Mada, possibly the only person on the planet whose name is spelled the same backward as forward. He is bubbling with excitement.

[Go to the next page.]

You tap him on the shoulder.

"What's going on?" you ask.

"It's about Dennis Krats and Edna Stark," he replies.

Uh-oh. Dennis Krats has been your best friend since kindergarten. Everyone knows that he's had a crush on Edna Stark for three years. And he's not the only one. Bob Barvess, a kid who has tried, without success, to swallow broken glass on two separate occasions, has also had a long-standing crush on Edna. The tension between Dennis and Bob has been building for years. Suddenly you know what's going on—a fight!

You push your way into the middle of the circle and, sure enough, there's Dennis. Pale, sweating profusely, and as unsteady on his feet as a tightrope walker with vertigo, he definitely does not look prepared for a fight. He looks more like he's suffering from a bad case of the flu. Dennis is many things— funny, loyal, trustworthy—but imposing he is not. If you were to draw Dennis as a stick figure, the picture wouldn't be far from reality. He is about eighty pounds … if he's holding a twenty-pound cinder block.

[Go to the next page.]

And then Dennis asks you the question that guys have asked each other since the beginning of time. Since professional wrestling became a thing. Since Julius Caesar ruled the Roman Empire. Since cavemen hunted wooly mammoths.

"You got my back, man?"

With Dennis awaiting your response, you search for Bob Barvess. But you can't find him. You do, however, notice a new teacher standing inside the circle. Strangely, this burly adult is doing nothing to break up the fight. Instead, he's just standing there, staring at Dennis and grinding his teeth.

You turn around and ask Adam, "Who's that?" nodding toward the teacher.

"Bob," he whispers dramatically. He seems terrified, and he's just a spectator!

If this were a movie, the scary, screeching music would now play, and the camera would zoom in on your face, capturing the horror and realization in your eyes. If it were an animated movie, your jaw would drop to the ground.

[Go to the next page.]

Bob is immense. He grew about six inches over the summer and clearly chose weightlifting camp over magic camp. And he could use a shave.

"You got my back, right?" Dennis asks you again, tears welling up in his eyes.

If this were a movie, you'd now have a bunch of flashbacks: to first grade, when Dennis kept it a secret that you peed yourself at the Museum of Water; to third grade, when Dennis spent an afternoon helping you search for the disappearing handkerchief, your favorite magic prop; and to last year, when Dennis took the blame for the fake rat incident.

But this is not a movie; there's no "pause" button. Bob is now lumbering in your general direction, and Dennis is pleading for an immediate answer from you.

[Go to the next page.]

And that's when it finally sinks in. The Cleveland Cavs have won an NBA title, the Chicago Cubs have won the World Series, and the world has generally been turned upside down. The old rules don't apply. It's a whole new ball game. Are you up to the challenge? Will you make the right decisions? Let's find out. ...

[If you have Dennis's back, in which case you two are in this fight together, turn to page 6.]
[If you melt into the crowd and root for Dennis from afar, turn to page 9.]

You respond, albeit not too convincingly, that you have his back. You feel sick to your stomach. Bob clenches his fist, raises his arm, and swings downward like a hammer trying to pound a nail. You dart one way, Dennis the other, and he narrowly misses both of you.

Suddenly the custodian, Mr. Dubois, is in the middle of the fight. "That's enough!" he yells. No kid would dare trifle with Mr. Dubois. Everyone, including Bob, disperses within seconds.

Mr. Dubois doesn't seem interested in reporting the fight to anyone who might mete out punishment, and moments later he is walking into the school whistling a Bruno Mars song.

"What was that all about? How did it start?" you ask Dennis.

"I told Edna that Bob is a total loser, and she told Bob what I said. And I stole his phone and dropped it in the toilet and he caught me."

"What?! Why did you do that? What did he do to you?" you ask.

"Nothing," says Dennis. "Also, I wanted to see if he would feel anything if I poked him in the arm with a safety pin, so I tried that when he wasn't looking."

[Go to the next page.]

There's a lot to be said for loyalty, but if you'd known the backstory you're not sure you would have had Dennis's back.

[Turn to page 11.]

Bob is a mountain of a middle schooler. This situation has an unmistakable *Game of Thrones* feel to it, and that's not good. As you step back into the crowd, Bob clenches his fist, raises his arm, and swings downward like a hammer trying to pound a nail. Dennis is the nail. Bob grazes Dennis's shoulder, but Dennis has dropped and rolled awkwardly, and it looks like he is okay. As Bob approaches, Dennis is on his knees combing the ground. What does he think he's going to find, a slingshot? With Bob just a couple of feet away, Dennis hurls a fistful of dirt at him. Luckily for Dennis, that fistful of dirt contains a rock, and that rock strikes Bob squarely on the nose, causing Bob's eyes to water involuntarily. Bob prepares for a counteroffensive, but the custodian, Mr. Dubois, breaks up the fight.

Miraculously, neither Bob nor Dennis faces disciplinary charges, and the account of Dennis's alleged victory spreads throughout the school with significant exaggeration. At recess, Leighton Rose shares breathlessly that Dennis slung a rock across the courtyard, clocked Bob on the head, and then gave him a wedgie while Bob cried and pleaded for mercy.

[Go to the next page.]

Dennis has a busy day retelling the story of that morning's fight and basking in his newfound popularity. But he also gives you a hard time for not coming to his defense. "I thought you'd get my back," he says.

You are still glad you didn't get involved, although never in a million years would you have predicted this outcome. This a common theme during the first few weeks of middle school: challenges are presented, and outcomes that were previously unimaginable somehow come to pass. Someone, you think, should write a fun book that gives middle schoolers the tools to analyze choices and their consequences.

[Turn to page 16.]

The next day you are sitting with your lunch crew: Rintu Chowdhury, Matt Thurber, Nolan Jacker, and Dennis. Instead of studying for your impending world geography test, you are focused on your meals. Matt brought chili, Dennis turkey, Nolan a salad with Russian dressing, and—oh no!—your mom forgot to pack you a lunch. You are really hungry, and you get in line for cafeteria glop.

When you return with your tray of mystery meatballs (what *are* those white chunks?), Rintu announces that your lunch group needs a name. After much deliberation, you decide to call yourselves the Mighty Awesome Power Squad (or MAPS).

Moments later Tamika Banks strolls over to your table, flanked by Leighton Rose and Valentina Lopez.

"Can we join you guys for lunch?" Tamika asks.

Is Frankfort the capital of Kentucky? Did the Pirates win the 1960 World Series? Is "pteronophobia" the fear of being tickled by feathers?

Yes, genius, the answer to all of those questions is "yes," and that's exactly how you respond to Tamika.

[Go to the next page.]

Tamika immediately suggests changing your group's name to Squad With Amazing Girls (or SWAG). Following some heated debate, the nine of you settle on "Squad." Squad-tagged pictures and DMs are soon filling up your Finsta feed. You must admit, it's fun to be part of a group—it's making the transition to middle school much easier.

Enter Marty McGrath, the most awkward kid you know. Marty lives and breathes dystopian books. *Divergent, The Maze Runner, The Giver*, and on and on and on. True, plenty of your friends really like these books, but they're basically *all* Marty talks about. His fixation can get really annoying.

One day he sits at your lunch table. "Imagine a world where humans are enslaved by fish and forced to work in oxygen factories at the bottom of the ocean," he says.

Everyone stares at him. No one responds. You look down uncomfortably at your tuna fish sandwich. The same basic sequence plays out again over the next two days. Eventually Marty gets the picture, gives up trying to draw people into his conversation, and goes back to his own lunch table, wherever that may be.

[Go to the next page.]

That night a stranger, "huxleyjr," somehow shows up in Squad's private group chat and starts insulting everyone:

"Dennis, you're more pathetic than Peeta."

"Valentina, you could never be a Nurturer."

When huxleyjr posts, "Imagine a world where anyone in a social clique gets quarantined on Mars," your suspicions are confirmed. You DM Marty: "Dude, what's up with you hacking our group chat?"

He responds, "Can't you stop playing these hunger games and just let me into Squad?"

So that's what it is. In his weird way, Marty is actually trying to make a connection. Or else he's being vengeful for feeling disconnected. Or both. Either way, you need to figure out what to do about it.

Marty doesn't have a mean bone in his body, so maybe you should just let him join your group. But then again, he's really annoying, and why mess with this Squad thing when it's working for you?

[If you tell Marty that he can't just force his way into a group of friends with a mysterious chat ID, turn to page 14.]

[If you try to get Marty into Squad, turn to page 15.]

No one is using shifty tactics to get into your group. Not on your watch. *You're* not asking to hang out with *his* friends. (Who are his friends, anyway? You're not quite sure.) Besides, if you let anyone who asks into an exclusive group, then what's the point of having an exclusive group in the first place? You message him your answer.

You: Marty, you have to leave Squad alone.

Marty: Fine. But when I start a colony on Mars, I'm going to totally recall this and exclude everyone in Squad.

You: Whatever.

Having set this precedent at the beginning of middle school, you spend the rest of middle school trying to leave people out of groups or get into groups yourself. Years later, you reflect on what a tremendous waste of energy this was. You can't help but wonder whether *you* were the mean kid in middle school. At your twenty-year reunion you find yourself apologizing to a lot of people for how you treated them. (Marty is not among them, as he's busy governing the first colony on Mars, to which you are not invited.)

THE END

You text the rest of Squad to discuss whether he can join. You all agree that it's an extremely important decision and should not be taken lightly. The initial response is that he is annoying and the odds will never be in his favor. But then Valentina recalls that he once missed his bus just so he could help her with her science homework. And Dennis points out that Marty is an amazing magician who performs tricks upon request. Huh, who knew? The other Squad members give in, Marty is in Squad, and he's genuinely happy about it.

He really *is* annoying but, truth be told, the other Squad members also get on your nerves at times. Half of Tamika's messages autocorrect to something unintelligible, like "I have a squirrelmeat but I can't share it with any of you." Nolan concludes every observation with the phrase, "You know what I'm sayin'." And every question Valentina asks feels like a trap. Two months later, the composition of Squad is completely different, and you wonder how the decision about whether to let Marty in seemed so important at the time.

[Turn to page 34.]

The next afternoon you are at Matt Thurber's house. The two of you sneak into his brother Frankie's room, where Matt introduces you to Frankie's bench press. He *literally* introduces you, telling the bench press your name. Then, pretending to be the bench press, he replies in a falsetto voice: "Hey, nice to meet you. Come give me a try. Look—just the bar, without any weights."

It's true, there aren't any weights on the bar, and didn't your grandmother just say how big and strong you've gotten?

You go through a mental checklist of your mother's "do nots": drugs, smoking, walking five miles until the public beach turns into a nude beach (ever again), etc. Weightlifting is not on the list and, in fact, your mom is always encouraging you to try new things and get more physical activity.

[If you give the bench press (just the bar) a shot, turn to page 17.]
[If you decline, turn to page 19.]

You lie down on the bench and, with Matt's help, lift the bar off the stand. No problem. Then Matt takes his hands off the bar and it falls to your chest. *This is forty-five pounds?* You can't lift it off your chest! Suddenly you are having trouble breathing. Your friend, who clearly had an inkling this was coming, is rolling on the floor in hysterics. You muster all of your strength and, your arms shaking, lift the bar ever so slowly, inch by inch, until you can finally set it back on the stand. The ordeal is over. Matt pauses his laughing fit, looks at you, says, "One," and then continues to laugh.

Is there a moral to the story? If so, you'll figure it out when you aren't so exhausted.

[Turn to page 18.]

[Turn to page 20.]

You pass on the bench press. Matt is extremely disappointed, which makes you suspicious. You try to curl some ten-pound dumbbells, but it's surprisingly difficult. You say goodbye to the weights until you've got a bit more meat on your bones. Mmm, meat. You need a grilled steak taco *right now*.

[Turn to page 29.]

That night you sit down at your desk, turn on the shared family laptop, and get started on your homework. Your first assignment is in social studies. Your research topic is "Richard Nixon: A Hard Man to Please." You start your research with the obvious search terms and, wait, what ... is ... that? Is it? It is. It's ...

[Go to the next page.]

PORN

Click here to see more, click here to see more.

[Go to the next page.]

You shake off some absolutely bizarre feelings and resist the intense temptation to "click here." You turn to your biology homework, which is to research organisms' asexual reproduction. Once again ...

[Go to the next page.]

<u>PORN</u>

Click here to see more, click here to see more.

[Go to the next page.]

With great resolve, you walk away, return five minutes later, and decide to tackle what will surely be safer topics, assigned in your two non-academic classes: in music class, a group research project on "the best sextets ever" and, in cooking class, a brief assignment on "hot grills." You guessed it …

[Go to the next page.]

Porn.

Is there any way out of this without just clicking? You know you want to. At least part of you does.

It sure seems that the internet gods have spoken and this path is somehow inevitable. Is it really even up to you? Your mom is nowhere nearby, and even if she knew how to check the browser history on the family computer (which you're pretty sure she doesn't), you know how to delete it. Anyway, a number of your friends have seen porn, so what's the big deal?

[If you "click here," turn to page 26.]
[If you don't click, turn to page 28.]

It's an itch that just must be searched—uh, scratched. You "click here." Your screen becomes covered in thumbnail video clips of men and women doing jaw-dropping *stuff* and unimaginable *things*. You're glad none of this is actually the subject of a report you have to write, since there is no way to articulate what's happening. The only way you could describe what's going on is in the negative—these people are definitely *not* playing Candyland.

You "click here" some more. Then you click there. You click everywhere. You can't stop. Three hours later, retinas burning, you shut everything down—but only because you think you hear your mom approaching. You barely sleep.

Sleep is the first casualty of your new fixation, but it is not the last. Sustenance puts up a bit of a fight, but it is sacrificed—when given the option, you choose to "click" instead of grabbing a glass of water to slake your thirst. Homework does not stand a chance; soon you are thoroughly neglecting your assignments.

[Go to the next page.]

A week later, you come to the realization that you are hooked. Even when all of the clicking leaves you feeling drained, empty, and sort of sick, you can't stop. When you do sleep, your dreams—which used to alternate between baseball and apple pie—are bizarre. Your grades suffer. As you learn a few years later when you start dating, your porn addiction has long-standing adverse consequences. You wish you had sought help way back when it all started, maybe from an older guy who might have understood what you were going through.

THE END

You're pretty sure you are using up your entire supply of willpower for the next ten years, but you do not "click here." A good thing, too, because apparently your mom is not computer illiterate. At dinner that night she asks you directly, "So what's the deal with all the porn site pop-ups on the computer?" You profess your innocence emphatically, and she tells you she believes you.

But after dinner she says she has a few more things to add. To your surprise, she still doesn't seem upset or freaked out, but it's clear she has a message to deliver. She tells you that you'll have access to porn for the rest of your life and that there's nothing she can do to stop you from watching it if you really want you. "But," she tells you, "most porn is completely unrealistic and a lot of it depicts violence toward women. If you're watching it, you're promoting it." Also, she notes that recent studies have shown that men who were addicted to porn as kids have trouble getting an erection when they are with actual women.

Not something you really want to hear from your mom, but you've got to hand it to her: she can really put things in perspective.

[Turn to page 49.]

In addition to sudden taco cravings, one thing that's different about middle school is that some of your classmates have begun standing up for a cause. Most of these causes, such as collecting money to buy a new cat for your school security guard, Mr. Binsinger, are sort of bland and certainly not very controversial. Others, such as Marty McGrath's Mars Colonization Association, seem random and far-fetched.

One cause, however, is both controversial and relevant, and that is Leighton Rose's club geared toward removing Mark Twain's *The Adventures of Huckleberry Finn* from the eighth grade language arts curriculum on account of its frequent use of the *n*-word. Leighton is dedicated and vocal and has amassed quite a following in support of her cause. She is pitted against Katherine Millihan, who has started a counter-club to keep *Huck Finn* in the curriculum. Katherine is equally dedicated to her cause.

If you're being totally honest with yourself, you don't really care all that much about this issue, and when they both approach you at lunch, you are far more interested in whether your PBJ has chunky or creamy peanut butter.

[Go to the next page.]

Leighton speaks up first: "You need to join my club. Racism has no place in our curriculum. Period. End of discussion. We can't tolerate the flimsy argument that 'that's just the way some people talked back then.' We cannot give a voice to racism and suggest that such divisive language is okay. With racial tensions worse than they've been in years, doing so is the last thing we need as a society. Anyway, we could just read the version that does not use racist language. You, of all people, should understand all of this."

What does she mean by "you, of all people"?

As soon as Leighton pauses to take a breath, Katherine seizes the opportunity to make her pitch: "You need to join my club. True, racism has no place in our society, but that doesn't mean we can't read a classic book just because it uses the *n*-word. It's important to view the language in its 1884 context and to acknowledge the reality of objectionable social behaviors from back then—while also noting that we now reject certain despicable habits of the past. Did you know that when the book was published, it was actually criticized for its portrayal of a close relationship between Huck and Jim?"

[Go to the next page.]

"Anyway, the most important thing is that we confront racism by reading and discussing the book, *not* by being afraid of words."

If she's not afraid of words, why did she refer to the "*n*-word"?

You smile at them both for no apparent reason. They do not smile back. They each want your support, and it's clear they aren't leaving until you agree to join one of their clubs.

[If you join Leighton's club, turn to page 32.]
[If you join Katherine's club, turn to page 33.]

You respond that you'll join Leighton's club and fight against *The Adventures of Huckleberry Finn*. Leighton is clearly pleased, while an unfazed Katherine simply finds another kid and begins making her case.

You attend the next club meeting (on Monday), meet some new people, and are proud to be part of a cause far more important than chunky versus creamy peanut butter. At the same time, you have your doubts about the stance this club is taking.

You never mention this to the other members of the club, but you have to admit that Katherine's arguments made some sense, and it occurs to you that perhaps the "right" stance on important issues is not always black and white.

You decide to try chunky peanut butter for the first time. It's pretty good! Hmm.

[Turn to page 148.]

You respond that you'll join Katherine's club and fight for *The Adventures of Huckleberry Finn*. Katherine is clearly pleased, while an unfazed Leighton simply finds another kid and begins making her case.

You attend the next club meeting (on Tuesday), meet some new people, and are proud to be part of a cause far more important than chunky versus creamy peanut butter.

You never mention this to the other members of the club, but you have to admit that Leighton's arguments made some sense, and it occurs to you that perhaps the "right" stance on important issues is not always black and white.

You decide to try creamy peanut butter for the first time. It's pretty good! Hmm.

[Turn to page 155.]

Your language arts teacher, Ms. Chang, is the nicest teacher you've ever had. She's tall and has short hair and a radiant smile that makes you wonder whether she shoots toothpaste commercials on the side. She is beautiful. You love her ... way of teaching. She has a particular affinity for poetry. Your assignment, should you choose to accept it (actually, there's no choice), is to write a poem about something inspiring and present it to the class. That night you work very hard to come up with the perfect poem to impress Ms. Chang, but the only thing you can think of is firecrackers.

Then you recall hearing about a poem that your great-grandfather wrote to your great-grandmother during World War II. You wander downstairs and ask your mom about it. She grins and retrieves a yellowed piece of paper from her special recipe box. You bring it upstairs and read it. It is really good. Why not just keep things simple and hand in this for your assignment? You weigh your options—the poem is by a family member, so you wouldn't be copying a famous poet or something. Also, it's either that or a haiku about firecrackers.

[If you write a haiku about firecrackers, turn to page 35.]
[If you use your great-grandfather's poem, turn to page 36.]

As much as you admire your great-grandfather's wordsmithery, you just don't feel right using his poem.

The next day, Ms. Chang calls on you first. Standing in front of the class, you close your eyes and recite your haiku:

Pop, hiss, crack, boom, bang
Flash powder or black powder
My explosive joy

The class stares blankly at you. You look at Ms. Chang. She is beaming. She does not profess her undying love for you (at least not yet), but that smile is enough to make you feel great.

You think it's a pretty good poem, certainly better than Rintu's five-minute limerick about flossing. You're glad you relied on your own creativity instead of filching your great-grandpa's work.

[Turn to page 37.]

The next day, Ms. Chang calls on you first. Standing in front of the class, you read the poem your great-grandfather wrote about seventy years ago. When you finish, Ms. Chang gives you a big smile, walks over to you, kisses you on the lips, and professes her undying love for you.

Okay, not exactly. Okay, not at all.

Actually, when you finish the poem, Ms. Chang says that it was a lovely piece but, before you sit down, she'd like to ask you a couple of questions. Where did you come up with the word "twitterpated," she wonders, and what did you mean by your reference to "storming the shores of Normandy"? You feel yourself getting hotter than a Roman candle.

When you have no response, Ms. Chang thanks you for the poem and asks the next student to present to the class. She never accuses you of plagiarism, and, in fact, when she returns your poem the next day, there's a scarlet *A+* at the top of it. Oddly, you were half-hoping for an *F*. Somehow the graded poem gets lost on your way home from school. Years later, you still feel your cheeks burning when you think about the whole incident and the *A+* you got.

[Turn to page 42.]

With a firecracker poem under your belt, you become increasingly interested in language arts. Your class is reading *Romeo and Juliet*. You're only halfway through, but you're enjoying your first Shakespeare play and have already predicted the ending, in which Romeo and Juliet will obviously run away together, raise a family, and live happily ever after.

At lunch, Rintu, Matt, Nolan, and you discuss Shakespeare's brilliant metaphors and explorations of universal truths about human nature. ... Well, not quite.

Rintu: My bro Bill knows how to roast.

Nolan: You mean William Shakespeare?

Rintu: Yeah, that bro.

Matt: Meh. He's nothing special.

You: Matt, thou art a fool and a coward.

The guys all laugh, and you are pretty proud that you remembered this. But Matt is prepared, recalling a line from the "Shakespearean Insults" game you played in class.

Matt: Oh, yeah? Thou art like a toad, ugly and venomous.

More laughter.

Nolan: Rintu, you speak yet you say nothing.

[Go to the next page.]

Rintu: A plague on your house!

Nolan: A bigger plague on your house!

Rintu: You, Nolan, are a man of wax.

Matt: Yeah, Nolan, you're so gay.

Really enjoying the back and forth, you are about to chime in by describing Nolan as "gayer than a bag full of rainbows," but before you have a chance to blurt out your line, the bell rings and interrupts the fun.

There's still time to get in the last word, but have you been saved by the bell?

[If you keep quiet, turn to page 39.]
[If you keep the conversation going, turn to page 40.]

You decide to keep quiet, and you're glad you do. The conversation goes pretty quickly from funny to nasty, from Shakespearean comedy to tragedy.

Nolan: You suck, Matt, and so do your insults.

Matt: See, you're not denying it.

Nolan: Right, I'm not denying that you suck.

Rintu: Come on, guys.

Nolan: You suck too, Rintu.

That's your cue: as tensions flare among your friends, you exit stage left. You will later learn that Nolan identifies as gay and has been figuring out for himself exactly what that means. Note to self: "gay" as an insult is not cool.

[Turn to page 144.]

You: You're gayer than a bag full of rainbows, Nolan.

Tremendous laughter.

But you've hit a nerve with Nolan, who, you will later learn, identifies as gay and has been in the process of figuring out for himself exactly what that means.

He responds by rattling off a string of swears directed at you. Even as things heat up, you can't help but be impressed with his ability to combine curse words in new and creative ways.

You: Chill out, Nolan, it's just a word. Shakespeare insulted people all the time.

Nolan: It's not the same!

Matt: He's all mad because he's all gay!

Not helping, Matt. Maybe Nolan will go after Matt instead. But Nolan turns toward you again and hurls a litany of expletives, the sort of expletives that, if included in a book for middle schoolers, would lead to worldwide protests and, in some countries, book burnings.

You: Nolan, dude, we're just teasing. Don't be such a baby.

Nolan: Okay, here's some teasing for you—at least I have a father. Where's your father these days?

[Go to the next page.]

Everyone looks at you. They know that Nolan has just taken the conversation to an entirely new level. Nolan is staring unapologetically at you. There is nothing you can say. It wasn't too long ago that it happened—memories of your father come flooding back. It hurts so much you are dizzy. You stumble away from your friends. It's a while before you recover.

THE END

What do a great white shark, a prowling lion, and a pack of middle school boys have in common? Well, yes, it's true that they all have eyes, but it's also true that when they smell blood they go in for the kill.

You're playing soccer at recess when it feels like a razor blade is cutting into your foot. The searing pain hits you so suddenly, you bellow in agony and rip off your shoe and sock. Your classmates huddle around you as you search for the razor blade. (It turns out to be a pebble. That evening you will attempt, unsuccessfully, to crush that pebble with a hammer.)

But something worse, much worse, happens: when you remove your sock you reveal your deepest, darkest secret, something you have managed to keep from your friends and classmates for years.

You have an extra toe.

Actually, it's more like a half toe, a pinkie on your pinkie. But it's there, with a toenail and all, for everyone to see. You quickly start to put your sock back on, but it's too late. Oh no, here comes the reaction …

"Cool," utters Dennis.

Others nod vigorously.

[Turn to page 44.]

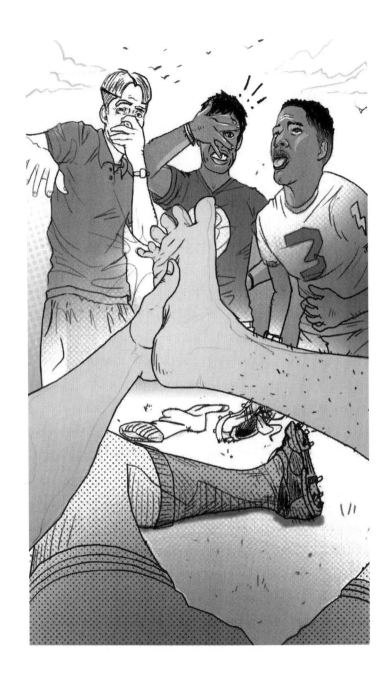

Well, that was close. Who knew your classmates could be so open-minded and see your half toe for what it is—a physical quirk that's really no big deal? (Years ago, you even considered it your special playmate and named it "Otto," but you were just a kid back then.)

Of course, all of your friends ask to see it again at recess. No sense in hiding it now. They are completely entranced. But then the sharks start circling.

Rintu touches your toe (without asking), recoils, and then runs shrieking to the other end of the courtyard for the full effect. Dennis wonders aloud how he's never noticed it before. Nolan asks whether it will fall off at some point. You explain that it's not like a loose tooth, but you can have a doctor remove it when you're fully grown, if you want to (and you may not want to).

There's a moment of silence. Then the tone abruptly shifts from curiosity to relentless heckling.

"This must be why you can't kick a soccer ball straight," Dennis says. Actually, your aim is remarkably accurate, but before you can protest, another barb comes your way.

[Go to the next page.]

Nolan says you should try out for the circus that's coming to town. He suggests you "put your best foot forward."

Rintu, now back from his run, declares that no woman will ever want to play footsie with you.

"What's it like to be retarded?" Matt asks.

They laugh uncontrollably, collect themselves, look at your foot, and all pretend to vomit.

And round and round they go—when it will stop, nobody knows.

How is this possible? These are your *friends*! Moreover, none of them is a stranger to being ridiculed. Completely overwhelmed, you do the only thing you can: you walk away. You are on the verge of tears.

At the end of the school day, you poke your head into the office of Ms. Martinez, the school counselor, as she's shutting down her computer and putting on her coat. Whether it's her big smile or the fact that she is considerably shorter than you, Ms. Martinez immediately puts you at ease. She asks you how everything's going and peppers you with questions about magic camp.

[Go to the next page.]

It is so nice to talk to her that you completely forget why you came to see her in the first place until she asks, "So, what's on your mind?"

You were here to talk about the half toe incident from this morning, but you're already in a better mood, and it seems as though you caught Ms. Martinez while she was leaving anyway. If you open up, your friends might get in trouble. And isn't this one of those situations where you just need to "be a man" and figure it out yourself?

[If you tell her you just wanted to say "hi" and then leave her office, turn to page 47.]
[If you keep talking to her, turn to page 48.]

You keep your emotions to yourself. Or, at least, you try. You bottle them up, but it's hard to keep the lid on them. You lock them in the freezer, but they somehow thaw. You bury them deep in your closet, but—let's face it—none of the metaphors you think up are helpful in getting past those feelings! You spend much of middle school frustrated and angry.

THE END

You begin telling your story slowly, but as the words start flowing, so do some tears. You tell her everything—much more than you've told your mom: a story comes out about the mean guy who measured your foot at Sole Cycle Shoes; you reveal the real reason you took up magic in the first place (to find a way to remove a half toe); and then you disclose the incident from earlier that day. It's a fifteen-minute conversation. Actually, more like a monologue—Ms. Martinez doesn't say a single word. (Her job must be *so* easy!) When you are done speaking, you stand up, thank her, and walk out of her office. You feel much, much better.

[Turn to page 174.]

Your after-school cooking class is taught in the cafeteria by Ms. Striker. Every Tuesday, she arrives precisely at 2:41 p.m., impeccably dressed in a suit, her gray hair pulled back in a tight bun, carrying an accordion folder of recipes and an expensive-looking leather bag of perfectly organized cooking implements.

Rumor has it that she used to work on Wall Street, trading derivatives or deriving trades or some such nonsense, until her doctor advised her to take up a less stressful vocation. It is unclear whether her doctor actually suggested that teaching middle schoolers how to cook would be a "less stressful vocation" for a total Type-A neat freak, but, well, yeah …

She is terrifying and constantly yells things like, "I've invested time with you people. I need to see returns!" and "If your calculations are off, even slightly, it could be catastrophic!" and "You, Goldman, if you're going to cook for your classmates, keep your hands out of the ingredients!"

Today is smoothie day. Everyone is supposed to use the designated ingredients—ice, milk, and peach slices—and follow the exact instructions provided by Ms. Striker to make a smoothie.

[Turn to page 51.]

Each of you will get to sample all of the smoothies, although with only three ingredients you can't imagine how they could possibly taste any different. But Ms. Striker is watching you like a hawk to ensure that there is no "human error."

As you go through the motions, Ms. Striker receives a phone call and has to rush into the hallway. Meanwhile, Leighton Rose opens the cafeteria refrigerator, and you spot a quart of almond milk, a bottle of vanilla extract, a jar of peanut butter, and a bag of kale lined up in a row. There's also a lonely potato on the second shelf.

You are suddenly intrigued. In your younger years, the only thing that captured your imagination as much as firecrackers was making "concoctions." When you were three, you combined water, dirt, and syrup. When you were six, it was chocolate milk, Cheerios, almond shavings, and syrup. When you were nine, it was oatmeal, pineapple juice, boysenberries, scallions, and syrup. Syrup has never lasted long in your house.

[Go to the next page.]

The almond milk, vanilla extract, peanut butter, and kale beckon you. (The potato you can do without.) Would using extra ingredients in your smoothie be breaking the rules? Or just harmlessly mixing things up a bit? Is the risk of Ms. Striker's wrath worth the creative rush of another concoction?

[If you grab the ingredients, add them in the blender, and see how it turns out, turn to page 53.]
[If you stick to the recipe, turn to page 54.]

Your cooking classmates watch with interest and mild concern as you resolve to shake up your shake. You marvel at your own dexterity—it takes you about twenty-five seconds to snag the desired ingredients, determine the appropriate amounts, and dump them in the blender. The neglected potato eyes you accusingly. You swagger back to your workstation.

Your classmates' remote interest turns to visible anxiety as they see Ms. Striker returning from her call.

You press "puree" in the nick of time, and the *whirrrrr* of your blender covers your tracks as Ms. Striker scans the room. Your classmates remain silent while you pour them their samples. Their eyes widen as they try it. "This is *really* good," their expressions say, and you are proud of your latest concoction. Your risk paid off in this case, although you'll have to be careful not to push your luck.

[Turn to page 69.]

It's just not worth the risk, you think. You follow Ms. Striker's directions and end up with a cup of boring peach slush that is indistinguishable from the rest of the so-called smoothies made by your classmates. Maybe you'll do batter next time. . . .

[Turn to page 88.]

The day ends on a bright note when you find an excuse to text Tamika Banks. Two days ago, a student set fire to a garbage can in the boys' bathroom. For some inexplicable reason, Principal Knivner wanted to chat with *you* about the incident.

Principal Knivner was a police officer for twenty-five years before becoming the head of your school. He's a gigantic man with large jowls and a neck almost as thick as his head. He speaks quietly, but somehow this only adds to the intimidation students feel when called into his office. He is renowned for his ability to spot a lie a mile away, and you have heard that kids who lie to him are treated more harshly than those who come clean. In this case, though, there's nothing to come clean about because you had absolutely nothing to do with the flaming garbage can. Knivner recognizes the truth immediately and wraps up the meeting quickly (even though you try to press him for details about the incident, hoping that there was a firecracker involved).

As a result of your meeting with Principal Knivner, you missed the language arts homework assignment. You decide to get it from the conscientious Tamika.

[Go to the next page.]

Your huge crush on her has absolutely nothing to do with this decision. Not a thing. Nada. You're just trying to follow your mom's advice and keep on top of your homework. And if that means a text message to Tamika, so be it. You spend fifteen minutes trying to think of an opening line, something clever and heartfelt, profound and yet a tad bit flirtatious, something that would make Shakespeare say, "Now there's a writer who's going places."

You begin: hey

She responds with equal brilliance: hey

You: what r u doing

Tamika: hanging out with friends

You: who

Tamika: friends

You: cool

Tamika: wanna see something

You: k

And then, to your amazement, there is a picture of Tamika. At least you're almost certain it's her. She's facing away from the camera, and her head isn't even visible. She's in her underwear. You have absolutely no idea what to say or do.

[Go to the next page.]

On the one hand, you recognize that the picture on your phone is invaluable for many, many reasons. On the other hand, if you had a nickel for every time you've heard about the dangers of pictures like this, you'd have two dollars because you've heard this warning exactly forty times. And then comes the game-changer text:

Tamika: u can show this to your friends if u want -tamica

Wow! Do you take Tamika up on her offer and show it to your friends? Your friends would be psyched, and it sounds like she's cool with that. And it's really no different from a picture of her in a bikini at the beach, right? Another option is to keep it but show it to no one, making this picture exchange just a thing between the two of you. Or you could delete it. But why?

[If you delete the text, turn to page 58.]
[If you show it to your friends, turn to page 59.]
[If you keep it but don't show it to anyone else, turn to page 62.]

Your Spidey sense is telling you that something is amiss—that you should delete the text. You do so, and it just feels right. Then, for the heck of it, you try to climb a wall. You make no progress, look ridiculous, and are forced to face the reality that you are not, in fact, Spiderman.

[Turn to page 111.]

You show Rintu the next day. He is floored and offers to trade you anything if you'll share the picture. When you refuse, he literally begs you to send him the picture and reminds you that he gives you gummy bears whenever he has them. You make him swear not to show it to anyone else.

In middle school, juicy pictures spread quicker than lice at a slumber party, and by that night a ton of people have seen Tamika in her underwear. You fall asleep with a dull ache in the pit of your stomach. With good reason.

The next day you don't even get through homeroom when you are called to Principal Knivner's officer. He is fuming. He shows you Tamika's picture on his phone. Clearly working hard to contain his rage, Principal Knivner asks you what you were thinking. You tell him that Tamika said it was okay. He asks to see your phone, so you hand it over.

"Did it ever occur to you that someone else probably took that picture of her?"

"No, sir."

"Not even when the text, which she did not write, by the way, said she was with friends?"

"No, sir."

[Turn to page 61.]

"How about the fact that she spelled her own name wrong? Was that a clue?"

Huh, how about that.

"No, sir."

"Tamika is devastated. Think about how you would feel if this were your picture all over social media. Last question: any idea why the truck from our local news station is parked in front of my school?"

You can guess why. But before you can stop yourself, you blurt out, "Am I going to be on TV?"

Principal Knivner is not amused.

"You are not, because I'm suspending you for a full week. Call your mom. She needs to pick you up."

When your mom picks you up, she's livid that you've "pulled a Tiger Woods."[1] Middle school just gets worse from that point on.

THE END

---

[1] "Pull a Tiger Woods": to send knuckleheaded text messages with major consequences.

You decide to play it cool and not show your friends. After science class the next day you say to Tamika, "Awesome text, T." See how you did that? You called her "T," even though that's not her nickname and no one has ever called her that before. You are oozing coolness.

"What are you talking about?" she asks.

"You know," you respond and, without another thought (seriously, you are *not thinking*), you pull out your phone and show her the picture. She is absolutely mortified. She grabs your phone, deletes the picture, and yells, "Did you send this to anyone?!"

"No," you tell her. You do not add that it's because you're so cool.

"Oh, my god, Kim must have taken this yesterday! I'm going to kill her!" She storms off. Well, that did not go as you'd hoped. At least she recognizes that it's not your fault.

Not so fast. Later that day you pass Valentina in the hall and she gives you the stink eye. Leighton ignores your texts. And the icing on the cake is that Kim Basta, who took and sent you the picture, calls you a disgusting pervert whenever she sees you. You are so confused!

[Go to the next page.]

Tamika doesn't speak to you for the rest of the year.

Also, you never got the language arts homework, so you ended up with a zero on that assignment.

THE END

Clyde is your mom's boyfriend. You don't have any issue with Clyde except that he's not your dad, but your dad's been gone three years, and you recognize that your mom should be able to date. You don't even mind that Clyde's job has something to do with parakeets, which sounds more like a hobby than gainful employment. In your opinion, you've been pretty accepting of him, all things considered.

Okay, you do have one issue with Clyde. Instead of using your name, he never fails to call you by a goofy nickname, and somehow he seems to have an endless supply of them. You've been addressed as Chief, Bud, Guy, Big Guy, Pal, Skipper, Skippy, Skip, Fella, Captain, Tiger, Ace, Boss, Kiddo, Partner, Sparky, Slick, Dude, and Mate. Where does he get this stuff? And how many more of these monikers can there be? You know he's probably just trying to be friendly, but you cringe every time he does this.

One Saturday afternoon, you, your mom, and Clyde are enjoying a minor league baseball game. Clyde is sitting in the middle seat, even though his ticket was for an outside seat. The conversation unfolds as follows:

[Go to the next page.]

Mom: Isn't it nice of Clyde to get these tickets for us?

You: Yeah. I just wish the cotton candy were a little more sugary.

Clyde: More sugary, Sport?

You: Yeah, you know, like having more sugar in it?

Mom: Sorry, you'll have to deal with the healthy cotton candy you have.

Clyde: So I heard you're dissecting a perch in science class, Doc. Whatdyathink? Gross, interesting, or a bit of both?

You: I dunno.

Mom (giving you an icy look): I think Clyde was asking because it's related to what he does for a living.

You: I thought you trained parakeets or something.

Clyde: Well, I'm a biomedical engineer, so . . .

You: Same thing.

(At this point you decide to stare straight ahead, focusing on the guy leading off first base, to avoid eye contact with your mom.)

[Go to the next page.]

Clyde stands up to get some food and asks cheerily, "You want anything, Bub?"

Sport. Doc. Bub. His nickname supply has no end. You've been cordial so far, but maybe it's time to put this guy in his place.

[If you politely ask for a pretzel, turn to page 67.]
[If you say something that will put Clyde in his place, turn to page 68.]

What's the point in calling him out? You politely ask for a pretzel. Your mom notices your change in tone and her icy expression softens.

The game turns out to be a good one. It goes to extra innings. It's difficult to stay quiet for three and a half hours, so you end up talking to Clyde. It turns out he grew up in Virginia, where fireworks are legal, and he has some riveting firecracker stories. You start calling him "Champ," which gets laughs from both him and your mom.

[Turn to page 140.]

"Yes, cotton candy, extra sugar," you respond. "And one more thing," you add. "Since you seem to know all of your parakeets' names, maybe you should know my name by now." You make a small show of reintroducing yourself, standing up to state your name clearly. Clyde just smiles and heads for the concession stand. From your mom, on the other hand, there are no smiles or concessions (the other kind). Instead, she launches into a tirade replete with guilt trips, threats, and pleas. By the time she's done, you feel pretty lousy.

THE END

Last school year seemed like an eternity ago, and your views on important world issues have changed since then. Your childlike devotion to Superman has given way to a deeper respect for Batman; you've forsaken the Patriots for the Giants (primarily because your mom is a huge Giants fan and you depend on this woman to feed you); and your steady support of the Cavs is nothing compared to your fierce new allegiance to the Warriors.

Your views on girls have also changed. Last year, if Tamika Banks had been dressed in a chicken costume and doing jumping jacks while singing "The Star-Spangled Banner," you would have walked right by her as though she were invisible. This year, she is suddenly noticeable, to say the least, and you have already walked into a wall on three separate occasions while passing her.

Many of your classmates seem to be in the same boat, becoming dazed and distracted by their crushes, and at some point Kim Basta and Hanbom Lee have started going out. It's unclear what that really means, although they've been spotted together at Mad Madeline's Ice Cream Parlor, so maybe that's all there is to it.

[Go to the next page.]

You wonder what would happen if you texted Tamika Banks, inviting her to Mad Madeline's. You have a huge crush on her and the timing just feels right, especially with after-school activities cancelled tomorrow.

It would be a bold move, but aren't Americans willing to boldly go where no one has gone before? You think of Lewis and Clark, Neil Armstrong, and Captain James T. Kirk. You are getting psyched up. Right on cue, your favorite song starts playing on Spotify. The world can't stop you; it can only try to contain you! You are the man!

With the adrenaline pumping, you craft the perfect text.

You: hey grab some ice cream at mad ms tmrw?

All you need to do is press "send." Do you have the guts to do it?

[If you send the text, turn to page 71.]
[If you hold off, turn to page 73.]

You do it, and you get an immediate response!

[To see Tamika's response, turn the page!]

Tamika: no

Ouch. You blame Kim and Hanbom for giving you false hope. You blame Lewis and Clark for setting an inimitable precedent. You blame your favorite song for getting you all pumped up. There's something to be said for not being afraid to fail, but it's even better when you actually succeed.

With undaunted courage, however, you push forward, asking for an explanation:

You: why not

Tamika: bc I have cashew practice

This cushions the blow of the initial "no," because at least the explanation is not "I really dislike you." Now if you could only figure out what word her phone autocorrected to "cashew."

THE END

You don't send the text because it doesn't seem like the right way to reveal your crush on Tamika. You can't help but wonder what would have happened if you'd sent it. Unfortunately, life is not an interactive story where you can go back and make the other choice, so you'll never know.

[Go to the next page.]

The next day the sun is shining and you can hardly wait for math class to end so that you can get to PE for some exercise. Apparently your PE teacher, Mr. Bussiere, has the same idea, because he has organized a timed one-mile run. You do pretty well. You're not sure what all the fuss is about breaking a four-minute mile. You've just broken an *eight*-minute mile—which is twice as much as a four-minute mile, right?—and yet no one is particularly impressed.

All middle school boys are supposed to shower after PE. But this is easier said than done. Whoever designed the middle school locker room was clearly waging a war on privacy, not to mention decor. The locker room consists entirely of:

1) a communal shower,

2) a communal bench,

3) a communal towel bin,

4) three sinks,

5) a stand-alone toilet *without any stall or covering whatsoever*, and

6) a single poster of the 1993 Montreal Expos, a baseball team that, you have learned, ceased to exist many years ago, possibly because the notion of facing an "Expo" failed to strike fear in the hearts of opponents.

[Turn to page 76.]

The mandatory shower rule has not been enforced, and most middle school boys, including you, have ignored it. But more and more of your friends are taking showers, and perhaps change is in the air.

Right now, however, something else is in the air, and that's the smell of you. You don't want to get naked in front of a bunch of people, but you can smell your own BO, and that stinks.

[If you shower, turn to page 77.]
[If you don't shower, turn to page 78.]

You strip down and shower with three other boys. All four of you have great difficulty finding the shampoo while trying hard to avoid looking (or looking like you're not looking) at one another. Even though your mom has told you a million times that there's nothing embarrassing about the human body, and you're sure that's true, you are still totally self-conscious from the beginning to the end of your first public shower. But it gets easier, and in a week's time you're oddly proud to be one of the kids who shows up to class with his hair still wet, like a recently showered Tom Brady being interviewed after a playoff game. Minus the interview and the playoff game and the five Super Bowl rings and the supermodel wife. But the good hygiene part is the same.

[Turn to page 99.]

You opt not to shower. You're just too self-conscious about being naked in public.

Later you notice that a couple of your classmates, including Tamika, seem to shift away from you in class. Dennis does not mince words: "Son, you stink."

Looks like you're going to have to deal with feeling self-conscious after all, especially when an unwanted guest, acne, soon arrives on your forehead and back because you don't shower enough. Live and learn.

[Turn to page 99.]

Since kindergarten you have been in school with the Strazza sisters, identical triplets you still have trouble telling apart. Sage, McKenna, and Calla Strazza have very different personalities. Sage is fun, McKenna is serious, and Calla is, well, totally unpredictable. This year they have all added a new article of clothing to their daily wardrobes—a bra.

Sage's bra has received the most attention because she is often involved in a hilarious game in which the boys try to snap her strap at recess. This is no easy feat—Sage is fast and seems to have eyes in the back of her head. The success rate is only about 10 percent, but that's what makes it so much fun. Sage laughs with any boys who are successful, but she laughs harder *at* any boys who are not. So far, you fall into the latter category, having tried and failed a number of times.

A chance to break your losing streak presents itself, however, when the bell rings to signal the start of recess and you see Sage duck into the girls' bathroom. You can hide next to the door and pounce when Sage comes out. But, wait, are you sure that's actually Sage, and not McKenna or Calla? You're not sure.

[Go to the next page.]

And you better get this right—because if it's McKenna she might get the wrong idea, and if it's Calla she might knock out your front teeth.

Luckily, the computer club is meeting in the next room over and you know for a fact that McKenna is the only one of the triplets in that club. So you're down to two possible Strazza sisters. What to do? You don't want to risk a trip to the dentist.

Then, in the distance, you spot . . . could it be? Yes, it's Calla Strazza on the monkey bars, wearing her signature braids. Suddenly a difficult choice seems easy.

[If you snap the third Strazza sister's bra when she comes out of the bathroom, turn to page 81.]
[If you don't, turn to page 83.]

The Strazza sister emerges. Your positioning against the wall is perfect. As she turns to walk in the opposite direction, you sneak up behind her and snap her bra. It *is* Sage—you win!

Nope, you lose.

Sage: Hey, what the heck do you think you're doing?!

You: Huh? I was, uh, you know, the recess game, um ...

Sage: I didn't say you could do that! That is not okay!

You are very confused, but you don't have time to sort out your thoughts because Sage heads straight to the school counselor, Ms. Martinez, who is nearby.

Ms. Martinez approaches you. You try to make small talk. "How's your cat, Ms. Martinez? I heard it broke its leg playing with a fan. Our feline friends are faced with lots of household dangers these days, am I right?" She is not fooled. She cuts to the chase and asks what prompted you to do what you just did.

As you try to explain yourself, it occurs to you that just because Sage has played the bra-snapping game before does not mean she authorized it in this case.

[Go to the next page.]

You realize that the question you should have asked yourself was not whether you had the correct Strazza sister, but whether any bra-snapping would have been a good idea.

To make matters worse, your mom and the Strazza sisters' mom are close friends, so the blowback from this incident extends beyond school.

THE END

You decide to hold off until it's clear that everyone is participating in the game. But that never happens because the school counselor, Ms. Martinez, gets wind of the game before it starts up. She pulls Sage aside and has a talk with her right there in the courtyard. You can't hear what they are saying, but Ms. Martinez is talking way more than she typically does, and Sage is nodding her head a lot. And that is the end of the bra-snapping game.

Though at first your decision next to the girls' bathroom felt like a lost opportunity, the more you think about it, the more the entire game seems problematic. You end up feeling satisfied that you chose wisely this time. You continue doing so as the year goes on, and middle school turns out to be terrific.

THE END

You are generally pretty honest, certainly more so than a lot of your classmates, as is clear during your math final. Though your eighty-five-year-old math teacher, Mr. Haller, has absolutely no idea, there is rampant cheating before, during, and after the exam. Perhaps his ability to see what's going on is obstructed by his enormous woolly bear caterpillar eyebrows. He seems surprisingly clueless for a guy who used to work as a government code breaker.

Your friend Dennis is among the kids who are brazenly asking others for the answers right in the middle of the test. You understand what's driving all of this—the test is difficult, and Mr. Haller is an unforgiving grader. Even so, it just seems so unfair that all of the kids who are cheating are going to do well and you might not, even though you studied really hard. You don't need to follow Dennis's lead exactly, but would it really hurt to sneak a peek at Katherine Millihan's test and see if she also got forty-five miles per hour for #13?

[If you take a quick peek, turn to page 85.]
[If you finish up your test without looking, turn to page 87.]

You casually glance over at her paper. Phew, she got forty-five miles per hour as well. When you look up, Mr. Haller is staring at you with laser focus. Did he catch you? You're not sure, but you think he may have, and now you're starting to sweat.

On the way home that afternoon, you are haunted by guilty thoughts and increasing certainty that you're going to fail the test, get expelled, and have to answer to your mother, who will surely accuse you of "pulling an Armstrong"[2] at least a dozen times. You barely sleep that night.

The next day you are on pins and needles. You dread math class and can't concentrate on any of your other classes all day. Finally, it's time for math. Your stomach does flips all period. Mr. Haller hands back the tests. Your test says *B+* without anything further.

But then Mr. Haller announces, "I am concerned about cheating on yesterday's test. I'd like to speak to the following students after class . . ."

[Go to the next page.]

---

[2] "Pull an Armstrong": to cheat to succeed, as disgraced cyclist Lance Armstrong did to win the Tour de France seven consecutive times from 1999 to 2005.

Haller's pause seems to last an eternity, and your heart leaps into your throat as you wait for him to name names. You're not the only one silently panicking.

Haller begins, "Mr. Krats." You feel bad for Dennis and the two other kids who are named, but you are relieved it's not you. You vow never to cheat again. Twenty-four hours of stress over problem #13 was just not worth it.

[Turn to page 123.]

You finish your test without looking at Katherine's and hand it in. Mr. Haller thanks you. You can't be sure, but you think he gives you a half wink.

The next day when you arrive to math class all of your desks are facing odd directions. Mr. Haller collects everyone's phone and hands out a piece of paper face down. He stands in the middle of the class and says, "You have twenty minutes. Begin!" You flip your paper over. It is a word-search game. Weird, but okay.

Most of your classmates look like they've just a seen a ghost. That's because most of your classmates didn't study, cheated, and are now getting their comeuppance in the form of a new test. You, on the other hand, are simply trying to find the word "pineapple."

"Good choice" is handwritten in the bottom left corner of the word search.

[Turn to page 119.]

You're not entirely sure where you fit into the social hierarchy, in middle school in general or even among your immediate group of friends. Much of the reason for this uncertainty is that your status seems to change on a daily basis. On some days you're the class clown with all eyes on you; other times, you just feel like you're on the outside looking in and it's all you can do to try to keep your friends (and yourself) out of trouble. One thing is for certain—you've never been at the top of the food chain.

But your fortune could soon change. You had a hat-trick in the soccer game last weekend, and there are rumors that two girls have a crush on you. Also, you recently came up with a phrase, "back to the brickyard," which all of the grade is now saying, even if no one (yourself included) really knows what it means. With a recent surge of confidence, you are poised to climb the social ladder.

On one of the rungs of the social ladder, you decide to pause and try your hand at some poetry. Here's what you write:

[Go to the next page.]

Fireworks of the World Unite

By You

When you are feeling down,
You can have both sight and sound
In the air or on the ground
It can turn your life around.

When the firework lights,
Your spirits reach new heights.
When it shows its might,
Everything's gonna be all right.

Some states still deprive
These feelings of being alive—
So shameful the ban:
Greatest invention of man!

This Fourth of July
With flags flying high
Unite, Young Turks!
Freedom to all fireworks!

[Go to the next page.]

You show the poem to your language arts teacher, Ms. Chang, and wait nervously while she reads. She smiles and describes it as "inspired." She gives you extra credit and asks whether she can share it with the class and post it on the bulletin board. You are proud. But you are also wary because being recognized as the middle school poet laureate is not exactly a road to popularity, and at the moment you are on that road. And, anyway, you didn't write it with the intention of anyone other than Ms. Chang reading it.

[If you let Ms. Chang share your poem, turn to page 91.]
[If you tell her you'd prefer not to share it, turn to page 92.]

You let her share the poem. It does indeed lead to some teasing, although several of your classmates also compliment you on your mad literary skills. You do not climb the social ladder any further, but it has nothing to do with the poem. Rather, the same day your poem is posted, Buzzy Van Dorn happens to use his most-feared-kid-in-school status as a bully pulpit to brand you as a "major loser" for no apparent reason, thus depriving you of further social advancement. That afternoon you are back to trying to avoid getting punched in the arm. Easy come, easy go.

[Turn to page 84.]

You thank Ms. Chang but pass on the public recognition. You do not climb the social ladder any further, however, because Buzzy Van Dorn has decided that you've climbed far enough. He tells everyone that you are a "major loser" for no apparent reason and boots you from the ladder to a chute. Before you know it, you are back to trying to avoid getting punched in the arm. Oh, well.

[Turn to page 174.]

For weeks you have passed by a foreboding poster that reads, "Mark Your Calendars: The Middle School Dance is October 15th!" And then you blink and it's October 14th. There is unprecedented drama leading up to the dance: boys asking girls and vice versa; a couple of girls asking girls; kids waiting in vain for responses; kids committing to go in groups; and kids begging parents not to chaperone.

In no time at all, it's October 15th and you are standing in the school gymnasium in a sports jacket that makes you feel like you just disembarked your yacht.

The dance, however, is surprisingly fantastic. The DJ takes requests from the kids. You ask him to play your favorite song. It is such a hit that two other kids request the same song! Most of the girls and some of the older boys spend almost the entire time dancing in a large circle.

You sit on the bleachers with your friends and punch one another in the arm, which is just fine with you. Life is simple, life is good, you think. And then you blink and it's not so simple.

[Go to the next page.]

The DJ announces that during the last fifteen minutes of the dance he will be playing a few slow songs to help wind things down.

The announcement takes both the boys and the girls by complete surprise, and there is absolute panic as all the kids try to find dance partners. The frenzy to pair up is like a puberty-themed version of musical chairs.

You are caught completely off guard. By the time you realize what is going on, just about every boy is standing close to a girl, trying to figure out how and where to hold onto her, the chaperones suddenly on high alert. You spot William Tramford, a smart brown-haired boy known for his remarkable knitting prowess. Seconds later, Tamika is holding his hand, heading toward the dance floor and visibly breathing a sigh of relief. Darn it! You are the only kid without a partner.

Well, not the only one. Lauren Somethingorother, who could easily be mistaken for a fourth grader, is also partnerless. This is not one of those situations, however, where the girl is staring at you and crying and you guiltily realize that you have no choice but to be her knight in shining armor.

[Turn to page 96.]

For one thing, while she is extremely nice, Lauren Somethingorother is not the crying type. For another thing, Lauren has facial blindness, which basically means that she doesn't recognize anyone who's not family, so even if she were staring right at you, she couldn't identify you.

You could easily spend the next fifteen minutes in the boys' bathroom, saving yourself from any humiliation. Moreover, if you ask Lauren to dance, she could either say, "Yes," which could hurt your chances with Tamika, or she could say, "No," which would be the most humiliating outcome by a long shot.

[If you head for the boys' bathroom and wait out the slow songs, turn to page 97.]
[If you ask Lauren Somethingorother to dance, turn to page 98.]

Sometimes when you find yourself in complete silence for an extended period of time, you think about your place in this vast universe, and a feeling of tranquility engulfs you. A virtual Zen moment.

Your fifteen minutes in the boys' bathroom brings you no such inner peace. The smell of smoke from Monday's garbage-can fire still lingers. You are doing your best to forget the unspeakable things that must have happened in the third stall tonight. And is that milk in the soap dispenser?

About twenty years later someone asks you to list the ten biggest mistakes you've ever made. Your "Give Piece a Chance" misspelled tattoo tops the list, of course, but your decision to hide in the boys' bathroom easily makes the list after you hear that Tom Brady Jr. has married Lauren Somethingorother, who also happens to be the US ambassador to Albania and the bestselling author of *And You Are? Living With Facial Blindness.*

THE END

You're overthinking this. You get off the bleachers, walk over to Lauren, and ask her to dance. To your amazement and humiliation, she says, "I don't dance."

But then she does. Together you sway back and forth. You talk about movies and end up in a funny debate about whether Chris Hemsworth is the actor who plays Captain America. (Wow, she really does have facial blindness.) It's extremely comfortable and actually pretty awesome.

And it's still comfortable and still awesome twenty-five years later when your kids are on the school bus, Lauren heads to work as the executive director of a nonprofit foundation, and you sit down to write another book for middle school kids whose parents are so great that they are sure to provide 5-star reviews.

THE END

It's your birthday! Happy birthday. Now go create a list of party attendees (limited to five boys) without hurting anyone's feelings. Your birthday celebration will start at Dave & Busters, and then you'll all head back to your place, where you'll watch *Guardians of the Galaxy Vol. 2*. Your longtime friends—Dennis, Rintu Chowdhury, and Matt Thurber—plus your new friend, Manny Miranda, are all sleeping over.

You're hooked on the soundtrack to the Broadway musical *Hamilton*. You've been listening to at least ten songs a day and have the entire soundtrack memorized. You've kept this to yourself thus far, concerned that even your closest friends might seize upon your newfound interest as an opportunity to ridicule you mercilessly. Not many middle school boys are into Broadway, and you're not really either—it's just that the *Hamilton* soundtrack is so unbelievably good.

But wait. Maybe these guys would appreciate this music, and then you'd have friends to join you in listening to the songs, which would be much more fun. Your birthday party could be your shot to share your interest with your friends (without any other classmates around).

[Go to the next page.]

Dave & Busters is a ton of fun, the movie is great (even though everyone has already seen it before), and now you're in your room with your buddies. It's your birthday and up to you to set the agenda. What comes next?

[If you start playing the Hamilton soundtrack, turn to page 101.]

[If you check your text messages instead, turn to page 102.]

You decide it's time and that this will be the room where it happens. You turn on the soundtrack.

Rintu (laughing): What the heck is this?

Matt: Is this hip-hop?

Manny: Can't we do something else? I'm already sick of this song.

You: Shh, talk less, listen more.

You notice that Dennis is mouthing the lyrics to "Ten Duel Commandments." Your friends walk around your room basically looking at your stuff, but no one asks that you turn off the music. Half an hour later, your mom comes to get you for cake. For a group of middle school boys who have spent hours together communicating primarily in grunts, this foray into a shared music experience has been all right.

[Turn to page 123.]

Playing it safe, you decide to keep *Hamilton* to yourself. You'll just have to wait to build up the nerve or find something else to share with good friends. But what will that be? Have you thrown away your shot?

[Turn to page 119.]

You are a very good soccer player, and this year people have started to notice. You are a starting midfielder and the youngest player on the middle school team. You are not the fastest or most skilled on the team, not by a long shot, but your soccer IQ is off the charts. If there were a Mensa society for soccer, you'd be in it. Somehow you are able to see how a play is going to develop long before it does. You lead the team in assists. You also lead the team in forgetting your jersey (your mom refers to this as "pulling a Chris Webber"[3]), but let's not talk about that.

With a record of 11–3, your team qualifies for the Middle School State Tournament. Your first game is against your regional rival, the Clinton Fighting Donkeys. They clobbered you 3–0 at the beginning of the season.

[Go to the next page.]

---

[3] "Pull a Chris Webber": to make a dumb mental mistake, such as by attempting to call a time-out when your team has none remaining, resulting in a technical foul that loses the 1993 NCAA Men's Basketball Championship game. Search "Webber Timeout" on YouTube.

You are unusually nervous the morning of the game. When you arrive at the field, your coach, Nicolae Ceaușescu Jr., takes one look at you and shakes his head. You are wearing a white t-shirt in lieu of your jersey, which is who-knows-where. He grabs some duct tape from his car. "Which number do you want, one or zero?" he asks. You request number one, of course. Although it requires a little extra effort, he tapes a large zero on your back. "Don't do this again," he says.

The exciting playoff atmosphere is palpable, and for once, a group of your classmates has shown up to watch. The game is a close one, 0–0 at halftime. With three minutes remaining, Matt Thurber crosses the ball from the right corner. You charge toward the goal and . . . completely whiff. In fairness, you were running full speed and it was a difficult ball, especially with your off foot. But apparently the crowd holds you to Cristiano Ronaldo standards because there is a collective groan from the sidelines when you miss the ball altogether. Your mom and her boyfriend, Clyde, are the only ones clapping encouragingly after you whiff, which makes the whole thing even more embarrassing.

[Go to the next page.]

The game isn't over, though. The Fighting Donkeys come down the other way, and with less than a minute left, their best striker sends a rocket toward your goal. It ricochets off the crossbar and starts a fast break for your team. You charge forward with your teammates as fast as you can. One of their defenders has ventured too far into offensive territory, and their goalie is completely out of position. Matt has the ball. With time about to expire, he floats a chip shot at their goal. It is a brilliant ball. You are sure that it will go over the goalie's head and land in the back of the net.

But a stubborn Fighting Donkey defender has other ideas. He punches the ball over the goal post, saving a goal. Handball. Penalty shot. The referee stops time as the other team tends to an injured player. Coach Ceaușescu calls your team over. There are only three seconds left in the game. Your coach breaks the silence: "Matt, you've earned the right. Want to take the penalty shot and win the game for us?"

Matt does not respond but his facial expression says it all—he clearly has no interest in taking the shot.

[Go to the next page.]

There is a lot at stake. You've managed to keep the game scoreless, but they have about twenty shots on goal to your three, and if your team misses the penalty shot and it goes to overtime, your chances are not good.

[Go to the next page.]

Coach Ceaușescu gives an understanding nod and turns to the rest of you.

"Okay, anyone else want to take the shot?"

[If you say you'll take the shot, turn to page 108.]
[If you keep quiet, turn to page 110.]

You look Coach Ceaușescu directly in the eye and say, "I'll make it." You step into the penalty box, position the ball on the grass the way you like it and, predicting that the goalie will dive one way or the other, strike the ball right down the center.

You are correct! The ball connects with the back of the net. Your teammates mob you, joined by the usually stoic Coach Ceaușescu, your mom, and Clyde. The school crowd rushes the field. You are lifted up on your teammates' shoulders. They drop you—*oof!*—but you don't care. It is the best feeling ever.

THE END

You are one of the best on your team at penalty shots, but you are really afraid to miss, especially after the whiff a few minutes ago. Will you be on ESPN's "Not Top Ten" if you miss? After what seems like an eternity, an eighth grader, Hal Avidarno, steps up and says he'll take the shot. A gangly, second-string defender, Hal wouldn't be your first choice, but there are no other takers, and you have to give him credit for being unafraid to fail.

Unfortunately, that courage does not translate into success, and he launches the ball about ten feet over the crossbar. The Fighting Donkeys score twice in overtime and your team is despondent. Would you have made the penalty shot? You'll never know. But you'll often wonder.

THE END

The next day your homeroom teacher hands out a "test" that will supposedly help determine the right career for you. This does not come as a surprise—your friends in other homerooms received the same thing earlier in the week. Of course they approached it with the utmost seriousness. Not!

They provided ridiculous answers. Dennis is headed for a career as a French hornist (though he would not know a French horn from French dressing); Matt, who is terrified of heights, will be a world-renowned, high-flying trapeze artist; and Rintu's test results simply read, "Odd Jobs."

No one will see the outcome of the test you are about to take other than you and your mom. Do you take the "test" seriously or follow in your friends' footsteps and botch it on purpose?

[If you provide accurate answers, turn to page 112.]
[If you provide goofy answers, turn to page 113.]

You take the test seriously. Your classmates do not. Everyone seems to be giggling as they fill in the bubbles on their answer sheets. Your results come back a few days later: "middle manager." What does that even mean? Is it because you're a midfielder on the soccer team? You show these enigmatic results to your mom.

"These things are so silly," she says. You didn't see that coming. Makes you wish you had just had some fun and filled in goofy answers.

[Turn to page 161.]

You fill in ridiculous answers, giggling along with your classmates. Your homeroom teacher, who is sipping an Extra Grandiose Starbucks coffee, either doesn't notice the class's antics or doesn't care. Your results come back a few days later: "parakeet trainer."

You show your mom and your mom's boyfriend, Clyde. The three of you can't stop laughing. Good thing you don't take everything seriously.

[Go to the next page.]

That afternoon, you spot an oddly forlorn Tamika Banks emerging from the nurse's office, carrying a stack of schoolbooks. Approaching her is Buzzy Van Dorn.

A word about Buzzy Van Dorn. In kindergarten, he teased you relentlessly about your Elmo lunchbox until you switched to brown paper bags. In first grade, he "accidentally" stepped on your diorama of the rain forest. In second grade, he stuck the sticker from his apple on your back twenty-one days in a row. In third grade, he started the deeply distressing lice rumor. In fourth grade, he pointed to you when the school librarian asked for volunteers to help restack books during recess (and you were chosen). Last year, he threw a football at your crotch (and he has good aim).

He has a buzz haircut, which makes sense, since he is basically a buzzsaw in sneakers, completely decimating everyone in his path. He has two large metal skull-and-crossbones earrings, which are clearly designed to make him look as menacing as possible. It works. He senses fear, preys on the weak, and has been bad to the bone since day one.

[Go to the next page.]

As he passes Tamika, he punches her schoolbooks out of her arms. He does it so naturally and nonchalantly that you think it's become an involuntary action for him, like breathing. Books and loose paper scatter all over the hall. Tamika is generally pretty tough, but something's off with her today, and she starts to cry.

Your blood boils. You hate Buzzy. Suddenly your rage turns to thoughts of revenge. They say revenge is a dish best served cold. Then again, they also say there's no time like the present. (Who is this "they" anyway, and why can't they get their messages straight?) Imagining yourself ordering a hot dish of revenge at a fancy restaurant, you come up with a brilliant scheme to get back at Buzzy for upsetting Tamika and for everything he's done to you in the past. To execute your plan, you need to get to a computer immediately. Tamika isn't making a sound, but tears continue to roll down her cheeks.

[If you unleash your ingenious plan, turn to page 116.]
[If you simply put your arm around Tamika, turn to page 118.]

In the past couple of days, you've learned three interesting facts about Buzzy. First, his real name is Buford. Second, he has a dog, a cockapoo named Dash. Third, he spends 85 percent of his waking hours on buzzfeed.com.

You have also recently discovered an app that allows you to create fake websites resembling real websites but with your own headlines. You find a computer and get to work. It doesn't take long before you have created a website that looks exactly like BuzzFeed, with the headline "Dash the Cockapoo Burned Alive in House Fire While Owner, Buford Van Dorn, at School." You date it today, track down Buzzy's phone number from Leighton Rose, and text him the link. It's only 10:30 a.m.—there's no doubt he'll see it before lunch.

He sees it by lunch, but by then Leighton has already told him you asked for his number, and he has already confirmed that the text came from you (and that Dash is safe and sound), so he is not the least bit fooled.

[Go to the next page.]

To the contrary, he is rip-roaring mad. You spend much of the rest of the week hiding in the custodian's closet. Looks like your "ingenious plan" was a misguided choice in disguise.

THE END

You walk up to Tamika and put your arm around her. Simple. To your surprise, she puts her arm around you. You walk down the hall like that. For all of your crazy schemes and failed attempts to get her to like you, this is all it took.

Years later, you are sitting on the beach with her, gazing at the sunset painting the horizon in reds and oranges. As your kids play in the water, you turn to her and ask for the thousandth time why she was in the nurse's office in the first place, but she still refuses to tell you. She says she prefers to think only of the happy times that began when you put your arm around her. Tough to argue with that.

THE END

It is a dark and stormy night, but the weather really doesn't matter when there is text drama, which there most certainly is tonight. And this time the spotlight is on you.

Valentina: I know somebody who likes one of u

Dennis: likes who

Valentina: not u

Rintu: me

Valentina: no

You: me

Valentina: ya

Rintu: who

Valentina: cant say

Dennis: is it ss

Valentina: no

Valentina: but maybe someone who looks just like her

You: calla

Valentina: y

Tamika: do u like her

Whoa, when did Tamika join? You don't know how to respond.

[Go to the next page.]

You: i dont know how to respond

Valentina: just tell us

You're not really interested in Calla, but you don't want to hurt anyone's feelings.

[If you say you might like her, turn to page 121.]
[If you say you don't like her, turn to page 122.]

You: idk

Valentina: so maybe

You: I guess

Sage: she likes u

You: sage have u been on this text the whole time

Sage: ya

Tamika: gtg dinner

Rintu: whats for dinner

Tamika: idk

Sage: calla says shell see u at school tmw

What just happened? It feels like you went for a haircut and had a kidney removed! Maybe honesty is the best policy, even when your good intentions tell you to avoid the truth.

[Turn to page 171.]

You: no

Valentina: why not

You: dinner gtg

Rintu: whats for dinner

Tamika: im bored lets keep texting

Sage: that wasnt very nice to calla

You: just being honest

Sage: maybe dont respond then

She has a point, especially since it's not always clear who's lurking in the e-shadows of a text chain.

[Turn to page 128.]

Since you turned ten, you have received a weekly allowance of ten dollars, provided that you complete your designated household tasks, which include taking out the garbage, folding laundry, and fixing the internet when it's down (which simply entails resetting the router, but your mom doesn't need to know that). You know from experience that if you shirk any of these responsibilities, the ten bucks will be forfeited.

In related news, parents at your school have managed to create a bake sale operation the likes of which the world has never seen. Located next to the security desk is a table with a never-ending supply of brownies and Rice Krispie treats awaiting any student with a dollar and a sweet tooth. You're pretty sure that if you were to break into the school at 3:25 a.m. on a Saturday, a smiling parent would be stationed at the bake sale table ready to sell you a cupcake.

[Go to the next page.]

Your mom has repeatedly grumbled that she's not thrilled with all of the sugar available, but since it raises money for the school, she won't "pull a George Brett"[4] on the parents who organize the bake sale table. That said, she's also not going to send you to school with money to buy more sugar—if you want to buy something from the bake sale table, you'll have to use your own money.

So you regularly do exactly that, as those homemade brownies are irresistible. One afternoon as you stop for your daily brownie, Rintu asks if you can get him one, too.

[Go to the next page.]

---

[4] "Pull a George Brett": to have a complete tantrum. Go to YouTube and search "George Brett." The "pine tar" video will be one of the first that comes up. Watch Brett's reaction when he's called out. Next time you are at a family event, pull aside any baseball fan over forty years old and say, "Remember the pine tar game of '83? Man, Brett's reaction was something else." When they are impressed with the incredible breadth of your baseball knowledge, tell them that you're just a student of history. Then ask them if they'll pay for your college education so that you can continue your lifelong pursuit of knowledge. The worst they can say is "No."

"Don't forget all those gummy bears I gave you a couple of days ago," he says. "And I'll pay you back tomorrow."

It's a nice thing to do for a friend, and he has been generous with his own junk food recently. You go ahead and buy him a brownie.

Rintu is duly awed when he takes his first bite. "These are delicious," he says. "Thanks!"

The next day you, Rintu, and Tamika are walking by the bake sale table again.

Rintu asks, "How about a brownie for Tamika and me?"

Tamika smiles. She's cute.

"Sure," you say. They are both very appreciative. You definitely scored some brownie points with Tamika.

Day three. Dennis joins Rintu, Tamika, and you at the bake sale table.

"Will you get me one, too?" Dennis chimes in.

He's assuming that you're buying for everyone. Rintu and Tamika do not disabuse him of this notion.

Brownies all around? Or tell your close friends that you're done feeding them?

[If you buy them all brownies, turn to page 126.]
[If you decline, turn to page 127.]

Remembering Tamika's reaction yesterday, you buy them all brownies. They thank you profusely, and it feels good. The next day Dennis buys you a Rice Krispie treat, but that gesture is offset by Leighton's appearance as a new, nonpaying member of your brownie entourage. By Friday, not only have you spent your week's allowance, you have also dipped into the money you had managed to save gradually over the previous month. You now have three dollars to your name. Is this the price of friendship? Maybe so, but something's gotta give or else your weekly labor at home will only support other people's sugar habits.

[Turn to page 189.]

You've had enough of using your hard-earned allowance to pay for treats for your friends. When you tell them as much, it comes out sounding a bit harsh. No one complains, but they don't look too happy, either. Dennis, in particular, is miffed. You're realizing there can be a fine line between a good friend and a sucker. Maybe set the ground rules a bit earlier next time?

[Turn to page 182.]

You have a secret you've never told anyone. Like the lifelong hunter who has never actually slain a defenseless animal, you have never actually set off a firecracker. It's not for lack of trying, but no matter how many ways you ask, your mom is resolute—no firecrackers. Yesterday she said that she doesn't want you to "pull a Pierre-Paul."[5] It seems as though she'll never grant your firecracker request. Middle school, and you've never even seen a live firecracker. But that all changes one fateful Friday night.

Soccer practice runs late and it is getting dark. You and Matt Thurber walk off the field together. You check your phone and see a text from your mom.

Mom: "Grandma's in the hospital. Going to be fine, but I've arranged for you to stay over at Matt's house tonight. I'll keep you posted. Love you."

You hope Grandma recovers quickly. In the meantime, hooray! Sleepover at Matt's! You ask him how you're getting there. It turns out his older brother, Frankie, will be picking you up in his new car.

[Go to the next page.]

---

[5] "Pull a Pierre-Paul": to destroy your hand setting off a firework, just as Giants defensive end Jason Pierre-Paul did on July 4, 2015.

When Frankie arrives, you see that "new car" is a relative term. The car is new in the sense that Frankie just got it, but old in the sense that it was manufactured before the invention of CDs and, apparently, comfort.

Frankie is joined by his best friend, Deuce. You know from Matt that Frankie has had his share of disciplinary issues, but he is an angel compared to Deuce, who bears a remarkable resemblance to Randall from *Monsters, Inc.*, and, as you are about to discover, identifies with the antagonist from *Stand by Me*.

When you get into the car, Deuce twists his head around the front seat and hisses at you, "So, boys, are you ready for some fun?"

Golly gee, some fun? Why, of course you're ready for some fun. That sounds swell.

You notice that Deuce has a baseball bat on his lap. Maybe you're going to the park to hit some ground balls. Oh, boy!

It turns out that the baseball bat is for knocking over mailboxes at a speed of about thirty miles per hour.

[Go to the next page.]

You and Matt watch wide-eyed as Deuce swings and connects with his mailbox targets time and again. He is very good at this "sport," and you surmise that he has played it before. The experience is both terrifying and exhilarating, and you and Matt just grin at each other while Deuce and Frankie holler and laugh.

"Okay, boys, next event," says Deuce. He pulls something out of his backpack. Something fantastic. Deuce has a bottle rocket.

It's true that sometimes your head is in the clouds. You once forgot your last name, and you still have to hold up your left hand in the shape of an *L* to make sure you know the difference between left and right. But you are pretty sure that you are the leading authority on the bottle rocket. In fact, you are a bit surprised that you have not yet been invited to be the keynote speaker at the National Pyrotechnic Festival in Tultepec, Mexico.

[Go to the next page.]

As everyone should know, a bottle rocket is a type of skyrocket. The "engine" is usually about two inches long and attached to a stick. The stick is placed in and stabilized by an empty bottle, which helps guide the rocket during the beginning of its flight pattern. Popular during the Hindu festival of Diwali, bottle rockets remain illegal in Canada and in several states, including your own. In Thailand's Isan region, Bang Fai rockets, which are essentially bottle rockets on steroids, can be sixty feet long and charged with up to a thousand pounds of powder. But you digress. In a nutshell, if someone offered you a choice between a twenty-cent bottle rocket and a puppy, you'd go with the bottle rocket.

The sound of a lit fuse snaps you out of your daydream. You see now that Deuce is holding the bottle rocket in his hand—but with no bottle!—and aiming it out the car window. It shoots into the night sky and erupts. He repeats this five or six times with the same result. It is spellbinding. Is this the single greatest night of your life? It could be.

[Go to the next page.]

Then Deuce looks at Matt. "Your turn," he says. A look of horror from Matt. A sneer from Deuce. The transfer of bottle rocket to Matt. The flame from a lighter. A lit fuse. *Hisssss* . . . holding the bottle rocket in his bare hand, Matt puts his arm out the window, aims at the sky, and, moments later, *boom*. Magical.

Your heart is pounding. You know what's coming. As Deuce fumbles in his bag, you notice an empty soda can near your feet. You pick it up, as you are not prepared to launch a bottle rocket from your bare hand. Deuce offers you a bottle rocket with his right hand, his lighter poised in his left. In the background, Katy Perry sings, "Baby, you're a firework! Come on, let your colors burst!"

[If you refuse to fire the bottle rocket, turn to page 134.]
[If you do fire it, turn to turn to page 135.]

You do something incredible. Like Neo when he sees the Matrix for exactly what it is, you are somehow able to slow down time, step outside of the situation in which you find yourself, and consider the choices and potential consequences. When you weigh all the bad things that might happen if you fire a bottle rocket from a moving car against the momentary thrill, the choice is clear. You say, firmly, "I don't want to." Deuce insults your manhood and continues with his pyrotechnic undertakings.

That summer you set off some fireworks with your Uncle Jorde. It is everything you always imagined, so spectacular that you write about it twenty years later, and your fireworks-inspired poetry earns you the Pulitzer Prize.

THE END

Your entire arm is shaking, but you manage to stick it out the window with plenty of time left on the fuse. You aim it at a forty-five-degree angle. Just as the bottle rocket is about to take off, you hit a small bump in the road that jostles your arm. The bottle rocket ignites and shoots off parallel to the ground, exploding above the windshield of a car traveling in the opposite direction.

You start hyperventilating. Even Deuce is thunderstruck. "Whoa," he reflects. For a split second you are gleeful, as it appears that you have impressed Deuce and everyone else in the car. But then terror and more terror, as you hear a siren. You have fired a bottle rocket at a police car while traveling at forty miles per hour.

Two months later, after numerous meetings with police, counselors, therapists, and school administrators, the single hardest moment of the entire ordeal is when your mother says, "I'm so disappointed in you. I guess I just couldn't raise you right all by myself."

THE END

The federal interest rate. The best brand of weed killer. Other people's sleep schedules. None of these topics interests you in the least, but you still find them infinitely more captivating than your body's circulatory, nervous, and respiratory systems. Unfortunately, your big biology test is on those three topics. Good thing it's a full week away.

You're in your room on a typical Tuesday night, listening to the kind of music that you like. Your mom is working late so you're home by yourself. You literally have nothing to do, no responsibilities. The rest of the week is packed with soccer practice and homework, including an important group social studies project. Come to think of it, the weekend is packed too, with two soccer games, a birthday party, and a visit from your grandparents. And isn't next Monday the middle school field trip? It is, and you won't be home until maybe 7:00 p.m.

[Go to the next page.]

Two conflicting thoughts cross your mind. One is that you should relax before things get crazy. The other is that this would be a good night to start studying for the science test a week away. Which thought will you put into action (or inaction)?

[If you start studying for the science test, turn to page 138.]

[If you take a break, turn to page 139.]

It is excruciatingly difficult, but you force yourself to open your science book and plod through the dense material. Distractions everywhere entice you—text messages *ping*ing on your phone, an old man's voice outside pleading for his dog to come back, sirens, a package at the door (which turns out to be a bag of dirt with a note that reads, "Grade A Ozark Mountain Dirt. Thanks for your interest, Ben. More to follow!"). Tuning all of this out, you remain calm and study on. You are turning off the light just as your mom walks in the door. What a miserable night—your studying almost doesn't seem worth the effort you've put into it, with the test still a week away.

But, alas, after a crazier week than you even expected, when you finally revisit science again on Sunday night, you discover that your miserable Tuesday night actually established the groundwork you needed to be ready for the science test. You are rewarded for your preparedness with an A.

THE END

You decide to clear your mind in hopes of putting yourself in a better position to be able to focus later. Three hours, forty likes, nineteen comments, five shares, and three new followers later, you are ready for bed.

Next Monday night arrives in a heartbeat. The bus picking you up from the field trip shows up an hour late, there's terrible traffic, and you aren't home until 8:30 p.m. By the time you've eaten and showered, it's 9:15 p.m. You crack open your biology book and do the best you can to cram as much information as possible into your head before you start falling asleep at your desk.

When your science teacher hands out the test the next day, she says, "Remember, this is almost half of your grade for the semester, so do a good job. It should take you the entire period."

Yikes. Your blood is pumping, and you are nervous and breathing hard. Unfortunately, you don't understand the biological processes by which any of these things are actually happening to your body, since you didn't study nearly enough. ... C-.

THE END

The next day you're in science class, learning about the animal kingdom. It's a beautiful day outside. The birds are chirping. The bees are buzzing. You are thinking about the birds and the bees. . . .

Tamika looks really good today. Focus, focus.

Your science teacher, Dr. Vigra, begins talking about pheromones. Focus, focus.

Tamika smells really good today. Focus, focus.

"When fully engorged with blood, a tick can be almost the size of a dime," Dr. Vigra explains. Focus, focus.

Has it been noted that Tamika looks really good today?

You lose one kind of focus and replace it with another, more carnal focus.

The bell rings and you stand to attention. Actually, you're already at attention because by now you have a raging erection that you're pretty sure is about to tear through your pants.

[Go to the next page.]

You sit down. Your heart is pounding, but it's still sending blood toward the culprit, which is threatening to make you the laughing stock of the school. You wisely wait for your classmates to leave, but there's still Dr. Vigra, and she has an "I want to be left alone" look.

Think, think, think. Yes, thinking itself may actually be the answer. You've heard that there are things you can think about to make an erection go away.

[If you think of a shriveled raisin in a giant yellow bowl, turn to page 142.]
[If you think of a turtle hiding in its shell from a polar bear in a blizzard, turn to page 143.]

The raisin-in-the-bowl mind trick does not help right away, but it does get you thinking about Jedi mind tricks. And that makes you wonder, once again, whether Luke is Rey's father. And that makes you think of your father. And, with the general letdown feeling that ensues, the erection problem is solved.

[Turn to page 103.]

Hmm, do turtles and polar bears even live in the same climate? This image is not doing it for you, nor is it diminishing your erection, which, if it could speak, would say, in a thick accent, "Buddy, I ain't goin' nowheres." Apparently your erection needs a grammar lesson, but that can wait until later.

You come up with two solutions to avoid total embarrassment. Unable to choose between them, you go with both. First, you pull a book from your backpack and, holding it as low as you can, pretend to read, which sadly ends up looking like you are trying to put your erection to sleep with a bedtime story. Then, you walk backwards out of the classroom so that Dr. Vigra can't see you from the front. On the way out you trip over a desk and fall on your butt.

"Are you okay?" Dr. Vigra asks, concerned. Your pride and butt are bruised, but everything else seems back to normal. You have to wonder which was worse: the erection, which is completely natural and happens to every middle school boy from time to time, or the absurd cover-up fail.

[*Turn to page 194.*]

That afternoon, you take advantage of your increased freedom by joining Matt and Dennis at Starbucks. You've never actually been to Starbucks before because there aren't any near you.

Just kidding, *that* would be crazy. There are three in your neighborhood, of course. It's just never been your cup of tea, so to speak. But here you are now, in line behind Matt and Dennis, unsure what to order. Other than the hot chocolate, the drinks are so complicated . . . and caffeinated . . . and you vaguely remember your mom mentioning a "no caffeinated or sugary drinks" policy.

Your friends can turn anything into a competition—who can eat the most salsa, whose socks smell the worst, who would be the best secretary of defense, and whose drink order is funniest. And thus begins the "Starbucks Coffee Ordering" competition.

Matt orders a coffee and gives the barista the name "Voldematt." He snickers at his own wit. So do you. The barista, a stout middle-aged man who looks like he's had one kid too many, wears a dull expression that says, "Really? Do you actually think you pioneered the fake Starbucks name?"

[Go to the next page.]

Dennis, however, is unfazed by the barista's utter lack of amusement. Laughing the entire time, he orders a double ristretto venti half-soy nonfat decaf organic chocolate brownie iced vanilla double-shot gingerbread Frappuccino, extra hot with foam whipped cream upside down double blended, one Sweet'N Low, one NutraSweet, and ice.

The three of you are in hysterics as the barista rolls his eyes while taking Dennis's $8.55. Then Matt turns to you with a suggestion—order a white espresso with caramel and give the name "Whitey." At that moment it seems like a hilarious idea.

And why not? True, it's a sugary, caffeinated drink that your mom has forbidden. And, of course, your name is not "Whitey," but all of this amounts to just a white(y) lie, right? And, yes, the barista is clearly irritated, and perhaps some people would find the term "Whitey" offensive, even racist, but could it really be that big of a deal? Are any of these issues actually compelling reasons to stop the fun?

[If you take Matt's suggestion, turn to page 146]
[If you just order a hot chocolate, turn to page 147.]

It's as hilarious as you had hoped, but a couple of years later you become a drug-addicted, racist serial killer as a direct result of your Starbucks order.

Okay, that doesn't happen—the only cereal killing that happens is your wolfing down a bowl of Rice Krispies later that day.

But there are some consequences of your espresso ordering, namely that you can't fall asleep that night. You count sheep. You count the frustrated beeps of the living room smoke alarm in need of a battery change. You count backwards from a thousand . . . and you get to zero! The last thing you remember before you finally fall asleep is glancing at the alarm clock—3:15 a.m. Team Caffeinated Sugar Drink 1, You 0.

You wake up the next day a zombie. You thought you knew sleep deprivation before, but it was nothing compared to this. You are so tired that you can't even lift the spoon to eat your Cheerios, which look like hundreds of eyes staring defiantly back at you. They'll stop doing that if they know what's good for them. Otherwise, they'll meet the same fate as last night's Rice Krispies. Wait, are you silently threatening your Cheerios? You really are exhausted.

[Turn to page 64.]

"One hot chocolate, please."

"Name?" the barista asks, a bit surprised at your plain vanilla order.

You give him your name. He writes it on the cup but it smudges immediately, so when your hot chocolate is ready they call out "Smudgy! Hot chocolate for Smudgy!"

You lost the "Starbucks Coffee Ordering" competition, but that's pretty funny.

[Turn to page 93.]

School ends, and you and Nolan Jacker walk around the corner to the Two Star Deli. Who was the marketing genius who chose Two Star over Three, Four, or Five Star Deli? Well, at least they were honest—the place is pretty grungy. A mangy black cat, Poe Boy, guards against mice . . . by licking himself in a corner next to rotting bananas.

When you enter, the store manager stares at you with the same suspicious look that you and your friends are used to by now. Why does everyone assume that tween boys are looking for trouble? So presumptuous, so unfair!

You pick up some batteries and read the back. They have zero grams of sugar, which is good. Nolan grabs three packs of a new kind of gum, Exuberance Explosion (peppermint flavored), and puts one back. Then he picks up two cans of Coke and, to your mutual delight, shakes them. You examine a chocolate bar that is 99 percent dark chocolate. Dark chocolate tastes like chalk to you, so you put the chalkolate bar back.

[Go to the next page.]

You look at Nolan, wondering if he's going to buy that gum soon so you can get going. Wait, rewind. Three packs minus one is two. Where did those other two packs of gum go?

The left arm of Nolan's baggy sweatshirt is a bit baggier than the right—he's stealing two packs of Exuberance Explosion!

"What are you doing?" you ask.

"Absolutely nothing," he says out of the corner of his mouth. "Just messing around with Coke." The look he gives you reveals an entirely different story . . . and a clear request, to keep your mouth shut.

There are many compelling reasons to do so. Both of Nolan's parents were recently laid off from work, so it's quite possible that he can't afford the $1.79 for a pack of gum. Would three bucks really matter to the Two Star Deli? And it's not as though Nolan's asking you to follow his lead or even shield him from the manager's view as he makes his way out of the store.

[Go to the next page.]

Your hands are clean (even if there is something gross stuck to the bottom of your shoe), and your friend has asked you not to betray him, so is there even a choice to be made here? Yep. . . .

[If you follow Nolan out of the store without a word, turn to page 151.]
[If you say, "Nolan, I think you need to put that gum back!" so that the store manager can hear you, turn to page 154.]

Glancing over your right shoulder as you leave the store, you notice a camera hanging from the ceiling. Then you look over your left shoulder and see Poe Boy staring back at you. Is it possible that one of his eyes is a miniature camera?

No, Poe Boy is not a cyborg cat. Maybe it's time to ease up on the spy movies. But that camera is worrisome. As you quickly turn a corner, you whisper to Nolan, "There was a camera on the ceiling." He becomes extremely agitated and pops a couple of pieces of gum in his mouth to calm his nerves. So much for returning the contraband.

A siren blares in the background. It's getting closer and closer. You walk faster and faster. If you were suddenly transported to the Olympic race walking finals, you'd both medal. A police car zooms by you.

And that's it. You go your separate ways, do your homework, play some *Grand Theft Auto*, and fall asleep.

The questions percolate overnight, and they are waiting for you the moment you open your eyes.

[Go to the next page.]

Stealing gum is a victimless crime because no one gets hurt, right? If so, how's stealing a car any different? Is the difference just the value of the item being stolen? Does it really matter that Nolan doesn't have much money? What is the population of Hazelwood, Oregon? (The last question somehow sneaks into the mix.)

While the deed is done, maybe it's not too late to ask Nolan some of these questions (except for the population of Hazelwood, Oregon, which you learn from a quick Google search is about twenty thousand).

[Turn to page 174.]

You speak up: "Nolan, I think you need to put that gum back!" You immediately regret it.

Nolan stops, looks at you with a combination of exasperation, disgust, and terror, and walks out. The store manager does not even hear you, as he's busy online buying *Surviving Middle School: An Interactive Story for Girls* for his fifth-grade daughter.

Nolan is long gone by the time you leave the store. But he's at school the next day and he's furious. He marches up to you before homeroom and yells, "You rat! Why did you do that? I could have gotten in huge trouble."

To your surprise, you invoke a vocabulary word from Unit Seven and respond, "I was trying to save you from becoming a kleptomaniac."

"What? Isn't that the plant that koalas eat? You're not making any sense." He shakes his head and storms off. He didn't study Unit Seven.

While you replay the scene at the Two Star Deli about a dozen times and think through how you might have handled it differently, Nolan never mentions it again, and there's no long-term impact on your friendship. But you are careful not to shop with him anymore.

[Turn to page 79.]

Dennis, Rintu Chowdhury, Adam Mada, and you are playing a game you all just invented called "Human Rock Target." Basically, one of you stands perfectly still about twenty feet away from everyone else. The other three sit on the curb and take turns throwing small rocks, trying to peg the standing person hard enough to sting but (hopefully) not to do any serious damage. And then everyone rotates positions.

The game is simple and brilliant, requiring only pebbles (or larger stones). And it seems like it will never get old!

And yet, forty-five minutes into the game, it *has* gotten old, and you are all completely bored. Then, on the horizon, movement.

Her high heels shimmer in the sunlight as her hips sway back and forth. Everything she's wearing is ultratight. Her black hair reaches to the small of her back. She looks like she's almost six feet tall. She's coming your way.

Rintu: Wow. We should pay her a compliment. Everyone likes a compliment.

Adam: There's no way I'm talking to her. She looks like a Victoria's Secret model.

[Turn to page 157.]

Dennis: You don't have to say anything. Just whistle. I've heard you whistle. You're an excellent whistler.

Adam: It is true, whistling is sort of my trademark.

Rintu: See, everyone likes a compliment. Let's all whistle.

Adam: Do you think she'll like it?

Dennis: Of course, it's a show of appreciation. If she didn't want to be whistled at, why'd she dress so hot?

They assume you're in. Join the group and pay this exceptionally attractive woman a compliment by whistling at her as she walks by you?

[If you whistle at her, turn to page 158.]
[If you don't whistle at her, turn to page 160.]

Rintu whistles, Dennis whistles, you whistle, Adam lets out an ear-piercing whistle, and then he yells, "Shake it, baby! That's what I'm talking about!" The woman is noticeably shaken and speeds away wearing a flustered expression. You all laugh, but it is an uncomfortable laugh because each of you feels partially responsible for taking things a bit too far.

What's done is done, though, and there's no use in dwelling on it, so off to soccer practice.

Your mom picks you up from soccer practice, bringing you a clean t-shirt for the ride home. As you walk back to the car, you realize that you've left your soccer jersey on the field, so you run back to get it. You grab it and jog to catch up with your mom.

Then, to your horror, you see three guys, probably in their late forties, approaching your mom. Are they parents of kids on your team? It's dusk and you can't tell. They look menacing. You pick up the pace, although you're too far away to prevent an attack.

[Go to the next page.]

They don't attack her, but one of them yells, "Hey, baby, why don't you bring some of that sugar over here?" The second guy says, "C'mon, honey, I like watching you walk away, but don't go." The third guy says something really vulgar.

Your mom says nothing. She does not even flinch. She just gets in the car, backs up, drives in your direction at a normal pace, stops the car, and tells you to hop in.

As you drive away, she's mutters something about our "Roethlisberger"[6] culture. One thing is clear from her reaction—this has happened to her many, many times before. You feel terrible for her and ashamed of your actions earlier in the day.

THE END

---

[6] Ben Roethlisberger: Pittsburgh Steelers quarterback accused of, but never charged with, rape.

You don't make a sound. Neither does Adam. Rintu lets out a halfhearted whistle. Dennis, however, yells, "Yeah, baby," in his best British accent. The woman literally spins around on a heel and walks up to Dennis who, you may recall, is about eighty pounds . . . if he's holding a twenty-pound cinder block.

"Thanks for the catcalling, boys. Keep up the good work. With your casual sexism and continued street harassment, more women can be on high alert whenever they pass a man. And it's great to see that you're starting at such a young age, paving the way for a new generation to objectify and scare women."

She swivels again and is on her way.

The four of you are speechless, but you didn't whistle, so, of course, the next words out of your mouth are, "Hey, Dennis, remember that time about fifteen seconds ago when that woman made a total fool out of you for being a sexist and you didn't have a response? Remember that?"

[Turn to page 11.]

Rintu and you have developed a surefire method of acquiring free ice cream cones. Not cones with ice cream, just the cones. Here's how it works:

Step 1: Find ice cream retailer with employee who looks like he or she would rather be anywhere else.

Step 2: Compliment employee's shirt, hair, or both.

Step 3: Inquire as to the cost of a one-scoop ice cream cone.

Step 4: Inquire as to the cost of one scoop in a cup. Inevitably the price is the same as a one-scoop ice cream cone.

Step 5: Appear quizzical, as though a brilliant thought is making its way to the forefront of your brain.

Step 6: Say, "Huh, so if the prices are the same, then the cones don't cost anything?" Inevitably the employee will agree with you, usually with a statement along the lines of "Uh, I guess so."

Step 7: Thank the employee for the clarification that cones are free. Request three free cones. Don't be greedy—request no more than three.

[Go to the next page.]

At this point the employee, having been backed into something of an analytical corner, will have three choices: 1) debate the logic of your position; 2) simply refuse to give you the cones without offering any reason; or 3) just give you the cones.

Step 8: If the employee chooses to engage you in a debate and wins (which is possible, especially if he or she focuses on the cost of a cup), concede defeat and move on. If the response is a simple refusal, push back by saying, "But you just said cones are free." If you are given the cones, consume the evidence ASAP!

Your success rate is about 85 percent.

And this, ladies and gentlemen, is how you plan to spend your two-week spring break—attempting to acquire free ice cream cones with Rintu.

Your mom, however, has other ideas. When you arrive home on the last day of school before spring break, there is an ancient man sitting on your couch.

[Go to the next page.]

He is wrinkled, withered, and wizened, and everything he does is at a snail's pace—it takes him about twenty seconds to reach for and grasp the cup of coffee in front of him, another fifteen seconds to bring it to his lips, ten seconds to drink, and another twenty-five seconds to return the cup to its coaster, which he squints to find. That sip of coffee took over a minute!

"Mr. Hobson lives down the street," your mom says, "and he's here to offer you a job during the break."

"Hello ... there ... young ... sir," Mr. Hobson begins. Twenty seconds.

"I ... am ... so ... happy ... to ... make ... your ... acquaintance ... I'm ... glad ... we'll ... be ... working ... together." Forty seconds.

What? He's making it sound like you don't have any choice. Your mom has set you up . . . brilliantly.

"Of ... course ... there ... are ... options ... which ... I've ... discussed ... with ... your ... mother ... weeding ... my ... garden ... or ... making ... phone ... calls ... for ..."

And then he stops and takes a sip of his coffee. Another minute! But his mind is sharp, and he picks up where he left off.

"... ten ... dollars ... an ... hour."

[Go to the next page.]

163

Looks like you'll be working a job this spring break no matter what. Hobson's choice. But you do get to decide which job. So what's it gonna to be, outdoor job or office job?

[If you hit the phones, turn to page 165.]
[If you hit the garden, turn to page 169.]

Talking on the phone for ten bucks an hour doesn't sound so bad. And then Mr. Hobson describes the job in more detail.

"You'll ... try ... to ... sell ... people ... pet ... insurance."

"Pet insurance?" you ask.

"Yes ... pet ... insurance," he whispers.

"You mean insurance for pets?" you ask, perplexed.

"That's ... right ... pet ... insurance," he answers.

"So, insurance covering pets," you say, still confused.

"*Yes, pet insurance, for crying out loud!*" he yells.

Basically, your job is to call strangers and remind them that Fido or Mittens or Nemo isn't going to live forever, ask them whether they have considered "preparing for the end," and, if they show interest or start asking you questions, politely put them on hold and hand the phone to Mr. Hobson.

[Go to the next page.]

You learn early on that people really don't like to be bothered, especially during dinner, and that they are generally not afraid to tell you so. You learn some new curse words. One guy suggests that you would be wise take out life insurance on yourself.

On your first day, Mr. Hobson sits in the same room with you, ready to take the phone if needed, but you wonder how that's going to happen since he's asleep in his chair. It never becomes an issue, though, because not a single person with whom you speak is interested. When you leave, Mr. Hobson commends you on a job well done, which you find odd, as you just experienced two straight hours of rejection.

On your second day, a woman concerned that Whiskers has already cheated death seven times and has therefore used up most of his nine lives wants to hear more. You put her on hold, rush to Mr. Hobson, and pat him on the shoulder to rouse him.

[Go to the next page.]

He wakes up a different man than the one you've come to know. With a twinkle in his eye and a noticeable spring in his step, he takes the phone and strikes up a conversation in which he is somehow both empathic and insistent, friendly and forceful. After fifteen minutes, he scribbles something on a notepad and hangs up. There is no doubt that the woman just purchased insurance for Whiskers.

"Where did you learn to do that?" you ask.

It turns out that during his extensive lifetime, Mr. Hobson has created and sold six different companies. His stories about his companies are riveting. So are those about his life in general. He won a silver medal at the 1960 Olympics, had dinner with Martin Luther King, invented the pet rock, fought in Vietnam, and helped save the American auto industry from collapse. You feel like you're chatting with Forrest Gump.

[Go to the next page.]

The next day you hand the phone to him twice. One ends in a sale, and he gives you a high five, which genuinely makes you feel good even though you are concerned that his arm will fall off. When he's asleep, you make calls, but when he's awake you are transfixed by his amazing stories.

At the end of the week, you start to worry that he's not going to pay you for all twenty hours you've been there, since you were only on the phone for about ten of them, but he hands you a check as you leave. It's for $300!

"Stop ... by ... anytime," he says. You will.

THE END

Pulling weeds is tough. Mr. Hobson says you're building character. Your mom says you're building character. But it feels like you are breaking back.

Your two hours of weeding on Monday are exhausting. Dirty and sweaty, you stumble into the shower and momentarily fall asleep standing up.

You start to get the hang of it by Tuesday, but this time you have to work for four hours, not two, and once again you collapse into bed that night.

Resigned to the job, you get better and better at it. By the end of the week, you're instantly able to distinguish between a weed and a plant, and you've developed a clever technique to grip a weed quickly and effectively. You have also become a master with a hoedag and any short-handled weeding tool. You even learn how to position yourself so that it doesn't hurt your back, and there are times when you actually feel sort of Zen as you lose yourself in weeding.

By Friday the garden looks great, and you're proud of what you've accomplished. You'd even forgotten that this was a paying gig, so it's actually a pleasant surprise when Mr. Hobson pays you $200.

And that's the last time you think about weeding . . .

[Go to the next page.]

. . . until seven years later, when you are a senior in high school awaiting the start of an interview at your first-choice college. The dean of admissions enters and begins the conversation by apologizing that she'll need to remain standing. "I spent the morning weeding my garden," she explains, "and my back is killing me. Any ideas?"

It's a rhetorical question, but, to her surprise and delight, you answer it confidently. When the acceptance letter arrives in the mail three days later, you think about the late Mr. Hobson and his garden.

THE END

Yesterday your barber asked you where you're from, and you answered, "San Andreas."

You've been playing a lot of *Grand Theft Auto V* lately (as Trevor Philips, who can give and take a beating like no one else). You're focused on your almost-completed mission and, motivated by that goal, you have cut down on *GTA*'s "extracurricular activities." You are close, really close.

Dennis calls while you are taking cover during a shootout. He wants to know if you want to play badminton.

"Ha ha, badminton," you say, although you're not entirely sure how one plays badminton.

"I'm serious," he says. "It's a lot of fun."

Why would you play badminton? You've already finished your homework, so you're not breaking any house rules by playing *GTA*, and you want to complete the mission you started three days ago. This is the time for perseverance, not giving up! You explain this to Dennis. He responds, less than convincingly, "Come on."

[If you finish the GTA mission you started, turn to page 172.]
[If you pause GTA to go play badminton, turn to page 173.]

The sunset paints the sky orange as you sit at your desk and complete the mission. Before you know it, you're onto the next mission and it's 11:00 p.m. You play more and more *GTA* as the year goes on. Your brain does not turn to complete mush as a result, nor do you become a violent criminal.

But remember the chicken fights at Adam's pool party, the mystery story you co-wrote with Tamika, and the coed hiking trip? No? Well, that's because all of it happened without you, while you were busy trying to upgrade your *GTA* vehicle. Just sayin' . . .

THE END

So here's the thing—badminton is astoundingly fun, and not just because the projectile used in the sport has the funniest name imaginable. You're really good, and you and your friends have discovered that it's still possible to talk some serious trash during a seemingly stuffy sport developed in the nineteenth century by the Duke of Beaufort.

Every night is a badminton battle, with the teams rotating. You and your friends are addicted— one night the temperature drops to freezing, and yet you play until the final game ends 33–31. You choose badminton over the World Series. You talk badminton every morning.

Your real badminton life is even better than your *GTA* virtual life, and it never leaves you with an all-night hangover or feeling disconnected from the real world around you.

THE END

If there is a universal middle school rite of passage, it may be truth or dare. You know for a fact that your parents played it in middle school and that their parents did as well. You wonder how far back the tradition goes. . . .

Middle School Kid: Truth or dare?

Middle School Neil Armstrong: Dare.

Middle School Kid: I dare you to go to the moon.

Middle School Kid: Truth or dare?

Middle School Cassius Clay (a.k.a. Muhammad Ali): Truth.

Middle School Kid: Do you really think you're so great?

Middle School Cassius Clay: I am the greatest!

Middle School John Adams: Truth or dare?

Middle School Thomas Jefferson: Dare.

Middle School John Adams: I dare you to declare independence from England.

Middle School Thomas Jefferson: Oh, come on! That would be treason.

Middle School John Adams: You said dare!

Middle School Thomas Jefferson: Fine.

[Go to the next page.]

You turn over this theory in your head: maybe American history unfolded as a giant nonstop game of truth or dare. You wisely keep this theory to yourself.

Among your friends, though, you have been doling out quite a few truth or dare questions recently, which you know full well means that you will soon be on the receiving end of one yourself.

That moment arrives in science class while you are learning about electricity. Sitting next to you, Rintu suddenly bolts upright, his eyes as wide as saucers, a figurative light bulb over his head. He smiles mischievously and passes you a note that simply says, "Truth or dare?"

You know from the look in his eye that he's got really good ones for both truth *and* dare. "Neither" is not an option. Oh man, this could end poorly. Pick your poison. . . .

[If you choose "truth," turn to page 176.]
[If you choose "dare," turn to page 179.]

You write, "Truth."

He passes the paper back to you: "Do you think Ms. Chang is hot?" That's a good one. Rintu knows it. You know it. You both know it. Because you both know the answer—an unqualified "Yes."

Do you write, "Yes," on the piece of paper and give it back to Rintu, or do you lie?

[If you tell the truth, turn to page 177.]
[If you lie, turn to page 178.]

"Yes."

You fold the piece of paper and sheepishly return it to Rintu. From his expression you'd think he had just won the lottery. He tucks it into his book bag. You pray that it never sees the light of day.

Your prayers go unanswered. A week later, Ms. Chang asks you stay after class. Please, please, please let it not be the note.

It's the note. She pulls it out of a folder. She doesn't have to open it. "I think we should keep these things to ourselves and focus on science in science class, okay?" she says, in a perfectly level tone.

Terribly embarrassed, you just nod your head and walk out of her classroom. You have a headache. They say sometimes the truth hurts. This is one of those times.

[Turn to page 64.]

"No," you lie.

You fold the piece of paper and sheepishly return it to Rintu. He glares at you and threatens to buy a lie detector and use it on you, furious that you didn't play by the rules. In this case, however, the rules required you to profess your lust for a teacher . . . in writing. You'll live with Rintu's ire for an afternoon, knowing full well that he'll be way more likely to spend his money on candy than to save up to buy a polygraph.

[Turn to page 55.]

The dare is this: "I know you're doing morning announcements tomorrow. I'll give you a script to read over the loudspeaker tomorrow before school."

The next morning, Rintu, grinning, gives you a paragraph he wrote the night before, the crux of which is a declaration that Earth has been invaded by Martians.

"You have to read it exactly the way I wrote it. Those are the rules of truth or dare," he reminds you.

Maybe everything will be fine and people will realize it's just a joke, you think. On the other hand, the entire school will be listening. . . .

[If you read the script, turn to page 180.]
[If you don't do it, turn to page 181.]

The next morning, you step up to the microphone in the main office and dutifully announce the school assembly details and the weather. And then, suddenly sweating, you read Rintu's script that says our planet is under alien attack and probably doomed.

You get through the entire thing before Assistant Principal Cruise emerges from her office and takes the microphone from you. Oh no, are *you* doomed?

"Heh heh heh," she chuckles earnestly. "Thank you! That was a very clever throwback to Orson Welles's 1938 *War of the Worlds* radio announcement. Of course, it was a joke then and it's a joke now, so let's not have mass panic. Now you have something to talk about in social studies class today," she says. She winks at you as she retreats into her office.

You have fulfilled an extremely tough dare without penalty. Sweet. But that was a close call, and you're *still* sweating. You know that there's just no guarantee of getting off so easily when pulling that kind of stunt.

[Turn to page 55.]

You're not willing to take the risk, even if it means incurring Rintu's ire for an afternoon.

Rintu isn't the only one of your friends with a strong sense of fairness, however, and a number of kids in your class give you a hard time for not following the rules of truth or dare. Eventually that dies down, but a couple of weeks later you say, "Truth or dare?" to Dennis, and he tells you that you can't expect to be taken seriously in that game anymore.

At first you are upset, but then you realize that it's not the end of the world.

[Turn to page 64.]

On Monday morning there's a new student in your class. Jean-Peter Leonard-Sartre heralds from Paris and is here as part of your school's new exchange program.

You and your classmates try, in vain, to figure out who it is you exchanged for him.

He speaks virtually no English and has a haircut that vaguely resembles a crashing wave. In your opinion, however, what stands out the most are Sartre's sartorial shortcomings—he wears a patterned silk shirt that is buttoned up to his chin and indoor soccer shoes that resemble the ones you've seen in pictures of your Uncle Jorde from way back when.

Dennis suggests that, since Sartre's name is long and difficult to pronounce, you should just call him "Frenchie." And most kids do.

"Did you see what Frenchie brought for lunch?" Nolan Jacker says one day. "That kid is weird."

"Tamika seems to like him well enough," says Rintu Chowdhury.

"His clothes are weird," you chime in, reflexively.

[Go to the next page.]

"We should prank him," Dennis says. You all stare at Frenchie, who, as usual, is eating with Ronny Descartes, a philosophical kid who speaks fluent French.

"What are you thinking?" asks Rintu.

"We'll pants him, of course," says Dennis.

Etymologists have traced the origins of the verb "to pants"—meaning "to forcibly remove another's trousers"—to 1980s parody films. But that's not important right now; what matters is the current motion to pants Frenchie. Rintu and Dennis vote in favor. Nolan abstains. You vote against, arguing that it may be a bit cruel.

But you've been outvoted. It is resolved—the pantsing will occur at 0800 hours tomorrow morning. Rintu will distract Frenchie with a giant green foam finger he'll bring to school (your friends' plots rarely make perfect sense) while Dennis attempts the pantsing. You are absolved of all responsibilities, which is fine with you.

But do you have a responsibility to tip off Frenchie about the impending pantsing, for the same reasons you voted against it?

[Go to the next page.]

Maybe not, since 1) you're not doing the pantsing, 2) it's a secret among your closest friends, and 3) Frenchie already has a friend who probably has his back.

[If you tip off Frenchie, turn to page 185.]
[If you don't tip off Frenchie, turn to page 187.]

You resolve to tell him what's coming. Given the language barrier, though, that's easier said than done. After an extensive and awkward pantomime (pantsomime?), you convey the point that he's in grave danger of being pantsed. He finally gets it. The next morning, he is nowhere to be found, and the pantsing plot fails.

In a clear (if uninvited) expression of gratitude, Frenchie joins you in the hallway between classes. You stumble through a conversation until you get to the topic of soccer, or rather football, as Frenchie calls it. Impressively, he knows every American star. At lunch you find a soccer ball and juggle together for half an hour.

At some point it occurs to you that maybe Frenchie doesn't like being called Frenchie. You decide to ask him. To your surprise, he says, choppily, that he doesn't mind it ("I . . . after all . . . French") but that he'd rather be called "Lorraine" because he's from the Alsace-Lorraine region in France. It takes you a while to figure out that he's joking.

[Go to the next page.]

You start calling him Jean-Peter from then on, and the two of you form a cool friendship, full of fascinating and increasingly comprehensible conversations, unlike any you've had before.

THE END

The Frenchie pantsing mission is successful, at least in the sense that Dennis and Rintu pull off his britches without any hitches, revealing to a large group of girls that Frenchie wears boxers covered with pictures of the Statue of Liberty.

Frenchie is mortified, but Dennis and Rintu apologize almost immediately, telling him that they were "just teasing." So everything's all right. Right?

Not so much. Frenchie hasn't a clue what they are saying, and you get the sense that, even if he did, the damage is done and can't be undone with a mere apology.

The situation goes from bad to worse for Frenchie. Whenever girls pass him in the hall, they strike a Statue of Liberty pose. Ronny Descartes decides to start eating lunch alone. Frenchie is miserable. Eventually the teachers get wind of the situation. You pass by the school counselor's office one day and catch a glimpse of Frenchie with his head in his hands just as the door is closing.

[Go to the next page.]

You feel terrible for Frenchie, but you have an idea. Maybe he could use a friend. You'll start hanging out with him more. You ask your mom to call Frenchie's host family to see if Frenchie can hang out, but she can't find their contact information.

Buzzy Van Dorn knocks Frenchie's books out of his hands one day, and you help him pick them up. Van Dorn sees this—you might as well have painted a target on your back. Now he tries to knock *your* books out of your hands.

Then one day Frenchie does not come to school. He's not there the next day either. Or the next. Or the next. In fact, you never see him again.

You imagine yourself making a speech to Dennis and Rintu about how saying someone is "weird" is just code for saying they are different, and that we should embrace, not shun, our differences. Patriotic music would play in the background. But you never actually make the speech. Instead, you find yourself guarding your books and wishing that middle school would just be over.

THE END

You've played the scenario over and over in your head a dozen times: it's a Tuesday after school, and one of your buddies approaches you with a sinister look in his eye. He opens his trench coat, pulls out a brand of cigarette called "Cancer Lite" and says, "Come on, dude, have a puff. All the cool kids are doing it. Try it."

Without hesitation, you respond, "Sorry, buddy of mine, study after study shows that smoking causes cancer. I reject your invitation to try the cigarette you offer me." You rattle off five more reasons why smoking is bad for you.

Your buddy says, "Wow, you're right. And so wise. And you smell great most of the time. I'm never going to smoke again. You've saved my life, bro."

Meantime, a smiling Tamika watches this interaction from a distance, impressed with your resistance to temptation and your noble efforts to save your friend's life.

One Wednesday morning, you arrive at school earlier than usual and you are greeted by Kim Basta, who at the moment is Tamika's best friend.

[Go to the next page.]

"Hey, look what my cousin gave me," she says, as she removes from her bag a handheld electronic device that vaporizes a flavored liquid. "Want to vape with me?" She adds, "Tamika is doing it," but she does not insist, threaten, or cajole. This is a no-pressure offer. In fact, seeing that you're unsure, she says, "You know what, go online and Google 'vaping is safe.' I'll have everything with me again tomorrow anyway." That's fair, you think, as Kim ducks into a corner of the courtyard so that she's completely out of sight.

You search that night and find several declarations from the all-knowing internet, such as, "Study Finds Conclusive Evidence that Vaping Is Safe," and "Holy Smoke! Vaping Is Safe, Even for Bystanders," and "Bill Mick Says Vaping Is Safe." Also, Tamika has a good head on her shoulders; there's no one you trust and respect (and have other feelings about) more than Tamika. Also, can't you take some comfort in the fact that this choice presented itself in a very different manner than the cigarette scenario you've played over and over in your head?

[If you join Kim the next morning, turn to page 191.]
[If you pass, turn to page 193.]

The next morning, you slink into the shadows with Kim, and she shows you how to vape. It's neither pleasant nor unpleasant, just weird. You don't get nauseous, so you try again the next day and the next. And you continue the experiment the next week, by which point you actually enjoy it. Kim lets you borrow some vaping accessories, including e-liquid, a charger, and an Eleaf iStick, which you hide in the inside pocket of your backpack.

One day you ask Kim why Tamika hasn't joined you.

"She said it's not for her," Kim answers.

"But I thought you said she's doing it?"

"No, I asked her to do it and she didn't want to."

You leave it at that, but later that day you Google "vaping is *not* safe." The word "e-cigarette" comes up everywhere, and you learn that e-cigarette fluid contains nicotine (along with propylene glycol, glycerin, and flavorings), making vaping highly addictive, just like smoking "normal" cigarettes. Health officials warn that, at best, the risks of e-cigarettes are unknown at this time.

[Go to the next page.]

Being a guinea pig for the vaping industry is not something you ever envisioned yourself doing. Fortunately, after just a few rendezvous with Kim, you are not addicted. So you give up vaping, cold turkey. Kim is surprisingly cool with your decision when you tell her one morning that you're done. All's well that ends well.

But actually, it does not end well, because you forget to return the vaping accessories you borrowed from Kim. As it happens, those travel advisories you seem to hear everywhere announcing that "bags are subject to random search" also apply at home.

And search, your mom does. And find, your mom does. And approach you with a look of anger and dismay, your mom does. And ground you for two weeks, your mom does.

THE END

One reason you refuse to vape with Kim is that you don't really know what you'd be getting into, and that gives you pause. Another reason is that, to you, "vapor" sounds like "viper" and "Vader," and those words invoke some unsettling images. Both reasons lead you down the right path, even if the best reason might be a different one altogether—the reality that e-cigarette fluid contains nicotine, making vaping highly addictive, just like smoking "normal" cigarettes.

Kim continues to recruit vape buddies. You never see Tamika with her, but Hanbom Lee signs up, clearly motivated by his longstanding romantic interest in Kim. The two of them and a few other kids live and breathe vaping. During the year you see less and less of Kim and her group, which becomes known as the "Nico Team," not the most flattering name. As far as you know, they never get into major trouble, although there are rumors that they start asking kids to "borrow" money to fund their "habit." (And that they use too many "air quotes.") Since you have been keeping your distance and hearing all of this secondhand, you remain unaffected. For you, middle school feels like a breath of fresh air.

THE END

It's a glorious Friday afternoon, and you, Matt, Nolan, and Rintu are sitting around admiring your own flatulence (a pastime you will remind Nolan of repeatedly after he becomes a US senator). When that activity gets old, you attempt to belch the alphabet. None of you can ever seem to get past *J*.

Then you turn to the always-good-for-a-laugh-or-two Human Rock Target. It's just one of those days when the four of you combined have the maturity of a two-year-old.

Matt pulls out his phone. You know what's coming next. The logical progression is from flatulence to belching to Human Rock Target to prank calls. Matt dials (718) 867-5309. He's clearly dialed this particular number before, and it must have some meaning. (You'll have to Google it later.) When an elderly woman answers, he asks for "Jenny." You hear the woman respond, "For the thousandth time, there's no Jenny here! You have the wrong number, Sonny!" The "Sonny" does it. You all roll on the ground in laughter, clutching your sides.

[Go to the next page.]

Rintu is next. He dials 1-800-DOGPOOP. When a monotone male voice answers, "Thanks for calling Jim's. We're the best at cleaning up Rex's messes," you all lose your—uh, composure—and laugh hysterically again.

You're up next. Your friends have two suggestions. Option 1 is to dial a completely random number, while option 2 is to call a florist and order flowers for your math teacher, Mathis Haller, who has an annoying habit of welcoming you to his classroom with the loud greeting, "Math is Haller!" Backing out of this seemingly harmless prank is *not* an option. What's it gonna be? One or two? One or two? One more time? Okay, one or two?

[If you dial a random number, turn to page 196.]
[If you order flowers for Mr. Haller, turn to page 198.]

You dial (501) 642-2323.

"Hello," answers a man with a distinctly Southern twang.

"This is Benjamin Dover," you say.

"Nice to speak with you today, Mr. Dover. I'm Lyndon Baines Jackson. Are you ready to order?"

Hmm, this is new, and you are unprepared. You friends await your response with bated breath. They are visibly disappointed when you repeat, "This is Benjamin Dover."

"So you mentioned. What's your address, Mr. Dover? I'll send you a free sample."

Maybe it's just an automatic response, but you rattle off your real address!

"Thank you, Ben. I appreciate the call. I don't get many requests anymore. If you want more, just call me back with a credit card."

"Huh, what?" you say, snapping out of a trance, but Lyndon Baines Jackson hangs up.

[Go to the next page.]

You don't know what to make of it, but your friends do—they erupt in laughter at your prank call fail and call you "Ben" for the rest of the week. Well, at least someone found it funny, and no one got hurt . . . but what's coming in the mail?

[Turn to page 136.]

You call Flowers At All Hours and ask for a dozen roses to be delivered to Mr. Haller. The woman on the phone asks how you'd like to pay and where you'd like them delivered. Quick on your feet, you provide the school address and answer that you'll pay when they arrive. There is a pause on the other end of the phone, and then the woman asks, "Are you Mathis Haller?"

"Yes," you lie.

Satisfied, she responds, "See you at nine tomorrow morning."

Your friends agree that you've taken prank calling to a whole new level, and they proceed, on Mr. Haller's behalf, to schedule the following deliveries and meetings for 9:00 a.m. the next day: three pizzas, a clown, and a remarkably gullible divorce attorney, all to be paid for by the recipient, one Mathis Haller. They give you credit as the trailblazer.

[Go to the next page.]

That night, however, you are not sure you want the credit, as it occurs to you that this prank call somehow morphed into a hoax that involves a bald-faced lie (you are not Mathis Haller) and people's livelihoods. You try to quell your anxiety by reminding yourself that sometimes in life you expect the worst and everything turns out okay.

[Turn to page 201.]

This is not one of those times. From your seat in art class, near the school entrance, you have a direct view of the scene that unfolds at 9:00 a.m. the next morning. A pizza delivery guy, a familiar-looking Barnaby the Clown, and a divorce lawyer walk into the school . . . and it's not the beginning of a bad joke; it's really happening before your eyes. Almost in unison, they announce to the burly security guard, Mr. Binsinger, that they are here for Mathis Haller. Mr. Binsinger refuses to let them pass. It seems like the worst is over.

Wrong again. Principal Knivner just happens to be walking down the hall at that very moment. He stops in his tracks and, upon seeing the increasingly testy clown, lawyer, and pizza delivery guy, sighs, shakes his head, enters the fray, and takes control of the situation. He pays for the pizza and shepherds Barnaby and the lawyer to the teachers' lounge, where they each grab a slice. It turns out that Barnaby is in the middle of a costly divorce, so they have something to talk about. You're out of the woods, right?

[Go to the next page.]

Not quite. Principal Knivner's ex-cop instincts kick in, he questions Barnaby and the lawyer while they eat their pizza and writes down some phone numbers, and fifteen minutes later an announcement is made over the loudspeaker that Matt, Nolan, and Rintu should make their way to his office immediately. Hopefully they won't implicate you.

Fat chance. Five minutes later your art teacher, Ms. Solomon, tells you with a solemn expression that you are wanted in Principal Knivner's office. When you arrive, it's clear that your friends have not only implicated you but, in your absence, portrayed you as the ringleader. Can this get any worse?

You've got to stop asking that kind of question! Each of you is suspended from school for "teacher harassment," and you have to call your mom at work to come pick you up immediately. Half an hour later, in an absurd twist that feels like something you've read in a book or seen on a sitcom, your highly-displeased mom arrives and recognizes Barnaby the Clown as your Uncle Jorde, who has been forced to work a second job to pay his legal bills.

THE END

Acknowledgments

My deepest gratitude to my fantastic editor, good friend, and partner-in-crime on various projects, Catherine Milligan.

Macy and Delilah, insert heartfelt mushiness here.

Kate, my sister, and John, my brother—you are hereby acknowledged! Again. So needy.

About the Author

Dave McGrail lives in New York City with his long-suffering wife, Lauren, and his wonderful daughters, Macy (ninth grade) and Delilah (fifth grade). He is also the author of *Surviving Middle School: An Interactive Story for Girls* and may or may not be the starting point guard for the New York Knicks.

70746294R00124

Made in the USA
Middletown, DE
16 April 2018